HELP!

All of a sudden a swirling ball of yellow sparks flew onto Hector's list and scrambled the letters into a new message. It said: I'm in BIG trouble now.

It was Ghostwriter, the team's invisible friend!

Jamal yanked his Ghostwriter pen from the holder around his neck. He fished a notebook from his backpack. He wrote: "What's wrong? What kind of trouble are you in, Ghostwriter?"

Seconds later, Ghostwriter's words appeared:

I'm not in trouble. A child wrote this. I think it's someone who needs help.

The Chocolate Bar Bust

by **Miranda Barry** and
Corinne Jacker

A Children's Television Workshop Book

Bantam Books
New York   Toronto   London   Sydney   Auckland

The Chocolate Bar Bust
A Bantam Book/May 1995

Ghostwriter, **Ghost**writer and ◉ are
trademarks of Children's Television Workshop.
All rights reserved. Used under authorization.

Thanks to SEGA and the ⚡ SEGA FOUNDATION
and to others who helped pay for GHOSTWRITER: public
television viewers, The Pew Charitable Trusts, the
Corporation for Public Broadcasting,
the Arthur Vining Davis Foundations,
the *NIKE*® Just Do It Fund, the John S. and James L. Knight
Foundation, and Children's Television Workshop.

Written by Miranda Barry and Corinne Jacker
Cover design by Marietta Anastassatos
Cover photo of brick building © Brent Bear/WESTLIGHT

ISBN 0-553-48287-4
Published simultaneously in the United States and Canada

PRINTED IN THE UNITED STATES OF AMERICA
OPM   0 9 8 7 6 5 4 3 2

Prologue

A hand reaches into a blue backpack, grabs a piece of white paper, and silently pulls it out. It's a list . . . a list of victims.

"This is going to make things a *lot* easier," says a voice, chuckling softly. Then a door slams and there are footsteps. In a second, the paper is folded up and stuffed into a pocket. No one sees a thing. . . .

Chapter 1

Door-to-Door Chocolate

"Listen, Hector, I *never* want to see a Jumbo chocolate bar again," Gaby Fernandez said to her friend and Ghostwriter teammate Hector Carrero.

In all of Gaby's ten years, she never thought she'd hear herself say those words. But she knew it was how everyone felt. The seven kids on the team were sick and tired of chocolate. And it was all Hector's fault. Ever since Hector entered the Jumbo Candy Bar Contest, he'd been begging them to buy more chocolate. Chocolate with almonds, chocolate with raisins, chocolate with peanut butter, chocolate with *chocolate*! Gaby suspected that even Hector was really sick of chocolate, but he was still his own best customer.

That was because nine-year-old Hector was desperate to go to swimming camp. It was an important step in his plan to become an Olympic swimming star. First prize in the contest was a scholarship to any sports camp the winner chose.

The contest had started one week ago, when school let out for summer. Time was running out— there were only two weeks left.

"I'd buy another, Hector, but I already spent my whole allowance on Jumbo Bars," said eight-year-old Casey. She looked at Hector sadly with her big brown eyes. Hector felt a little stab of guilt.

"You've got to get yourself some new customers, man," said Casey's thirteen-year-old cousin, Jamal Jenkins. He flopped back on the couch in Hector's living room, where the team had gathered to hang out and listen to music.

"I know," Hector said glumly. "Look at this." He pulled a piece of paper from the back pocket of his jams. The headline said: JUMBO CANDY BAR SALES CONTEST. A long list showed how many candy bars kids in the contest had already sold. The name at the top was Keisha Brock. Hector's name was second.

All the kids groaned when they saw the list. Keisha did just about everything well, and adults loved her. What they didn't know was that the nine-year-old girl who was so sweet and polite to them was downright mean to other kids.

"If you looked up *poor sport* in the dictionary you'd see a picture of Keisha," said Gaby's big brother, Alex. "I feel for you, Hector."

"Yeah, but I do have a new plan to sell more ca—" Hector stopped talking in midsentence. A ball of swirling yellow sparks had materialized from thin air and was scrambling the letters on the contest list into a new message: I'm in BIG trouble now.

It was Ghostwriter, the team's invisible friend. The kids weren't sure who Ghostwriter had been when he was alive. But they knew he looked out for them and could sense their feelings. Ghostwriter couldn't talk, but he could send messages in writing, and he could read words the team wrote to him. Ghostwriter had first contacted Jamal by entering his computer and sending him messages on the screen. He had made himself known to the other six kids on the team one by one. The kids had formed the team because they were the only ones who could see Ghostwriter's glowing messages.

Jamal yanked his Ghostwriter pen from the holder around his neck. He fished a notebook from his backpack. He wrote: "What's wrong? What kind of trouble are you in, Ghostwriter?"

Seconds later, Ghostwriter's words appeared: *I'm* not in trouble. A child wrote this. I think it's someone who needs help.

"That's not much information to go on," Alex said.

"Ask Ghostwriter if he can read any other clues near the kid," Lenni Frazier said excitedly.

Jamal wrote the question, and Ghostwriter brought back more writing: June 12th— Conrad got so mad at me for losing it. I wish I had someone to talk to about this. I'm so far away from home. I'm scared.

"The kid says someone named Conrad is really mad at him for losing something," Jamal said as he copied both messages into his notebook.

"But we don't know what's missing," Gaby added.

"There's a date on the message—June twelfth. That's today. Maybe it's from a diary," said Alex.

"You're right," said twelve-year-old Lenni. "And it sounds like that kid is in trouble. We should try to help."

"But we don't have any evidence yet," Jamal said. "Let's keep our eyes open for trouble. Ghostwriter will bring us clues when he finds them."

"Speaking of trouble," Hector cut in, "Don't forget that I'm having chocolate bar trouble.

"Let me tell you my new idea," he went on. "I've decided to sell Jumbo Bars door-to-door."

Hector held up a card with a string attached. "It's a special card I made to hang on doors when customers aren't home. It's got my name and telephone number in case no one is home when I stop by. Then they can call me and I can go back later to sell them the candy."

The team didn't look convinced. Hector ran into the front hall. The team heard him open a closet and begin rummaging around. There was a loud thump, followed by a muffled "Ouch!" from Hector. "I'm okay," he called a second later. He came back into the living room with his hair all messed up and some lint stuck to one shoulder. He was holding a big piece of poster board.

"Look what I made last night. How about *this* as a visual aid?" he said. The giant poster's headline was: FIVE GREAT REASONS YOU SHOULD BUY A JUMBO BAR FROM HECTOR TODAY.

Underneath was written:

1. I'm not leaving until you buy one.
2. You'll save yourself a long walk to the store.
3. Jumbo Bars come in four choco-licious flavors.
4. Jumbo Bars cost less than a ride on the subway, and they taste better, too!
5. The cute kid holding this sign could win a scholarship to sports camp.

Casey, who loved silly humor, read the first reason aloud and then hooted with glee. Soon the entire team was reading aloud and laughing.

Jamal got a thoughtful look on his face as the laughter finally died down. "Hector, that poster is really cool," he said. "But it's not a good idea to sell candy door-to-door. Something bad could happen to you."

Alex nodded. "Most of the people in our neighborhood are nice," he said, "but you can't tell who's behind a door if you've never been there before. It could be dangerous."

"I know," said Gaby. "What if you try selling just to older people? They'd probably like to have a kid come visit, and they'd be glad to help out by buying a Jumbo Bar." Gaby had worked in a volunteer program with senior citizens the summer before.

"Yeah, but how can I find them?" Hector asked, sounding frustrated.

"Try thinking of people you already know." Tina Nguyen spoke up. "Then they can give you the names of their friends, and soon you'll have a whole lot of people to sell to."

"Yes!" Hector said. "That's a great idea, Tina."

Eleven-year-old Tina flicked back her long black hair and grinned proudly.

Hector tried to think of older people he knew.

Right away, he pictured Mr. Yafa. Hector's mother had made bookshelves for him last month and Hector liked him a lot. He was like a second grandfather to Hector, whose real grandparents lived in Puerto Rico.

Whenever Mr. Yafa saw Hector, he asked Hector to tell a riddle. And he was already one of Hector's best Jumbo Bar customers. Two days ago he had bought six Jumbo Bars for himself and his daughter and all her kids.

"I can try out my new sales pitch on Mr. Yafa," Hector declared. "When he sees my poster, I bet he'll buy six more bars!"

"Okay, but how about if I go with you?" said Jamal, who was big for his age. "At least at the start."

The next morning, Hector and Jamal went to Mr. Yafa's apartment building. Mr. Yafa buzzed them in, and the boys took the elevator up to his apartment.

When Hector and Jamal were standing at Mr. Yafa's door, Hector ran his hand through his short black hair and brushed off his shirt.

"You look great," Jamal said. "Go for it."

"I feel great," said Hector, his brown eyes shining with excitement. "That scholarship is as good as mine. Watch this. Mr. Yafa loves my riddles."

Hector rang the bell. He had a big smile on his face when the door opened.

"Hey, Mr. Yafa. What's big and round and—"

Hector took one look at Mr. Yafa and stopped. Mr. Yafa looked terrible. His face was pale and his eyes were red, as if he'd been crying. His hands were trembling as he motioned Hector and Jamal inside.

"Mr. Yafa!" Hector exclaimed. "What happened?"

Chapter 2

A Bogus Bill

The boys followed Mr. Yafa into his apartment and helped him sit on the sofa.

"What's wrong, Mr. Yafa?" Hector asked again. "Are you sick?"

Mr. Yafa still couldn't speak, but he shook his head.

"Did you get some bad news?" Jamal asked, bringing him a glass of water.

After a few sips, Mr. Yafa was able to talk. "Something awful happened to me this morning. It's the worst thing since my wife died. I don't know what to do."

Mr. Yafa told the boys he'd been planning a trip

to California to see his grandson graduate from high school. That's why he'd bought so many chocolate bars—they were presents for the family.

"I had all the money saved up and was going to buy the plane ticket today. But I'm not going now. Not for graduation—not *any* time."

"Why not?" Jamal asked. "Weren't there any seats on the plane?"

"No, that's not it. It's that all my money's gone."

"Did somebody break in?" Jamal asked.

"Were you mugged?" Hector asked. "We know a police officer, Lieutenant McQuade. We can call him."

"No, boys. It was a bill I had to pay, a big bill. I didn't even know I owed it."

Jamal nodded. "People forget and get behind in the rent."

"No," Mr. Yafa insisted, "it was a new bill, a *water* bill, for over seven hundred dollars! Some woman from the City came to the door and said I had to pay for my whole year's water. In cash. Or the City was going to throw me out of my apartment."

Hector looked at Jamal. "That's terrible! I wonder if my mother got one of these bills, too."

"Well," Mr. Yafa said, "maybe she didn't get one because she's not on social security." He explained that when a person turns sixty-five, the government starts sending him or her money every month.

"Is social security like welfare?" Hector asked.

"Not exactly," Mr. Yafa replied. "People pay the government money while they are younger and working, so that when they retire money will come *from* the government to pay for rent and food and things."

"I get it," Hector said.

"But what about your big bill?" Jamal asked.

Mr. Yafa continued with his story. "The lady who gave me the bill said I get money from the government, so now I have to pay the City for all the water I use. My friend Betty Washington told me she had to pay four hundred thirty dollars to someone who came to her building to collect for the same thing."

Hector put his arm around the old man's slumped shoulders. He offered him a free Jumbo Bar with raisins, but Mr. Yafa shook his head. "It's not just California. The bill was so big that I don't even have any money to pay my rent now. I'm going to end up being thrown out of my apartment." Mr. Yafa buried his head in his hands.

"We're going to help you, Mr. Yafa," Jamal said. "We'll talk to my grandma CeCe. She'll know where you can get help with your rent money."

"This is my home," cried Mr. Yafa. "I don't have anywhere else to go. I'm going to become an old street person, sleeping in a doorway somewhere!"

"No, you're not," Hector said firmly, but he felt scared.

"Not if we have anything to say about it," added Jamal. "We're going to see my grandma right now, and we'll come back later to see how you are."

As soon as the boys left Mr. Yafa's apartment, they raced toward Jamal's house to talk to his grandmother. Halfway there, Hector heard someone call his name. It was Keisha, sitting at the table she'd set up in front of the supermarket, and she had a huge grin on her face. "Hey, Hector, I just sold another eight Jumbo Bars," she called. "What about you? Did you give up yet?"

Hector ignored her. "Did you see that, Jamal?" he grumbled after they passed. "She doesn't just want to win. She wants *me* to *lose*. She's crazy."

"Forget about her, Hector," Jamal said. "Right now we've got to try to help Mr. Yafa."

Jamal's grandmother had just come home from her job as a mail carrier for the Post Office. She had changed into a caftan made from a colorful African print and was just sitting down in the living room with a new novel. Jamal got her a glass of iced tea and the boys sat down and began to tell her about Mr. Yafa's troubles.

As Grandma CeCe listened, the frown on her face got deeper and deeper. "Water bills?" she finally said. "Are you *sure* he said he had to pay a *water* bill?"

Jamal and Hector nodded. "That doesn't sound right to me," Grandma CeCe said, shaking her head. "In New York, people who rent apartments don't have to pay for their water. And it sure doesn't make sense that old people on social security should have to pay for water when many other people don't."

"And why would the City make him pay all at once, in cash, instead of sending him a bill?" Jamal asked.

"You're right, Jamal. That's not the way the City does things," Grandma CeCe said. "When the City wants to collect money, it sends a bill in the mail. I deliver them all the time."

Hector suddenly looked very worried. "Do you think someone tried to cheat Mr. Yafa, made him pay a fake bill?"

"That's exactly what I'm afraid of, Hector," said Grandma CeCe. "But don't you worry, honey. I've got some friends in high places and nobody is going to put Mr. Yafa on the street if I have anything to say about it."

The boys went outside and sat on Jamal's stoop to think about what Grandma CeCe had said.

"I think this is a case," Hector said. "It sounds like someone ripped off Mr. Yafa with a fake bill."

"Yeah. That's what's called a con artist—a person

who gets money by lying—like this person who handed out a fake bill," Jamal said.

"Let's call a rally and get the whole team in on this," said Hector. Jamal opened his notebook and wrote "Rally J" on a blank page. Within seconds, the letters jumped off the page and started to swirl in the air. Ghostwriter was carrying the message to the rest of the team, telling them to meet at Jamal's house.

Ten minutes later, everyone was on Jamal's front stoop.

"What's up?" asked Lenni who was wearing a big straw hat and funky striped tights. Lenni liked to wear "interesting" clothes.

The team listened as Jamal and Hector told them about the water bill Mr. Yafa had paid.

"I think we should go to Mr. Yafa's right now and ask him some questions," said Lenni, thoughtfully running her finger along the brim of her hat. "We need more information about the person who collected money from him." The team agreed and took off for Mr. Yafa's.

When Mr. Yafa opened his door this time, he had washed his face and he wore a clean shirt.

"No point in sitting around moping," he declared.

Then he noticed that there were five kids standing behind Hector and Jamal.

"Hector, is this a party no one told me about?" Mr. Yafa said. The kids could tell he was trying to be cheerful, but he still looked shaken and pale.

"Mr. Yafa, these are my friends, Tina, Alex, Gaby, Casey, and Lenni. You already know Jamal. We all want to help you."

Mr. Yafa looked surprised, but Jamal quickly explained: "My grandma CeCe knows a lot of people at City Hall. She said she's not going to let anyone evict you, even if you can't pay your rent. But we want to ask you more about this bill collector. We think it was a con artist, collecting a fake bill."

"You mean you think this person cheated me?" Mr. Yafa looked as if he was about to cry again.

"It's possible," said Jamal. "Grandma CeCe said she doesn't think New York gives water bills to people who rent apartments."

Then Mr. Yafa looked angry and embarrassed. "I know I'm getting old, but I never thought I was getting stupid, too!"

"You're not," Hector protested. "It isn't stupid to be fooled by a criminal!"

"But now we need the best description you can give us of the person who gave you that bill," said Tina.

Mr. Yafa thought for a long time, and then he

said, "She was not young—but she wasn't old either. I can't tell how thin she was, because she was wearing a big sweater. She had brownish hair in a kind of bun, but the thing I remember most about her was her voice. She had a very strong Southern accent, so strong that I had trouble understanding what she said. But I did hear her say I had to pay the bill or I'd be kicked out of my apartment."

Jamal copied the information into the team's casebook. The casebook was a notebook in which the team listed evidence and clues about crimes. The new page read:

SUSPECT—MR. YAFA'S BILL COLLECTOR
Woman
Brownish hair
Big sweater
Southern accent

EVIDENCE
Collected over $700 from Mr. Yafa

Jamal put out his hand. "Can I see the bill?"

"I don't have it. She took it back with my money," Mr. Yafa said.

Jamal remembered that Mr. Yafa said his friend had also paid a big water bill.

"What was Mrs. Washington's bill collector like?" Jamal asked.

"All she told me was that he had a German accent," Mr. Yafa replied. Jamal added that information to the casebook. He jotted down his phone number and gave it to Mr. Yafa. "Please call Hector or me if you remember anything else, okay?"

"Sure," Mr. Yafa said. "I'm so thankful for everything you want to do for me. I only wish I could do something for you."

"You could tell me how to sell more candy, Mr. Yafa. It's really important if I'm ever going to make it to the Olympics," Hector said. "My swimming teacher at the YMCA says I'm built like a fish," he added, flexing the muscles in one thin arm.

"A minnow, right?" teased Lenni. She gave his arm a playful swat and smiled.

Mr. Yafa smiled, too. "If only I had some money, I would buy a case of Jumbo Bars from a good kid like you, Hector."

"Well, maybe some of your friends would feel the same way?" Hector suggested. He told Mr. Yafa about his plan to sell the candy door-to-door.

Mr. Yafa laughed and patted Hector on the back. "Selling the bars door-to-door is a good idea. It's the American way—start small and soon you're a captain of industry."

"I don't know," Jamal said. "I don't like the idea of Hector's ringing a lot of strangers' doorbells."

"That's smart thinking, Jamal," Mr. Yafa agreed, rubbing his chin with his hand while he thought. Suddenly his eyes brightened. He bustled off into the bedroom, leaving the team members in the doorway exchanging puzzled glances. When he came back, Mr. Yafa was unfolding a piece of paper with a list of names and addresses on it.

"The Community Center put together a group of older people," he explained. "Instead of cooking our noon meal, we get it delivered to us. That way we're sure to get our vegetables. We call it the Lunch Bunch. I got this list of all the members last year when I wanted to invite everybody to a holiday party. These are all nice older people who would love to have a visit from a fine young businessman like Hector. They aren't rich, but they can spare a dollar or two to help send a boy to camp!"

Hector thanked Mr. Yafa at least five times before the team could pull him away. They left Mr. Yafa standing in the doorway with a big smile on his face. "Helping you win your dream makes me feel a lot more hopeful!" he called as the kids got on the elevator.

Back at Jamal's house, the team thought about what to do next.

"Why don't we write to Ghostwriter and see if he can find Mr. Yafa's water bill?" Lenni suggested. "Without it, we don't have any real evidence."

Jamal wrote the note. Several minutes passed before Ghostwriter came back with a weird message:

CITY OF NEW YO
Broo
WATER BILL
IAM YAFA......................$73

Jamal quickly copied it into the casebook. "Some of the letters are missing," he said when he was done writing.

"That first line is probably 'City of New *York*,'" Hector said, and Casey added, "I bet the next word is 'Broo*klyn*.'"

"Good, Casey!" Jamal said, proud that his younger cousin from Detroit was getting to be such a sharp member of the team.

"Look at the money due," Hector said. "It says seventy-three dollars, but Mr. Yafa said his bill was more than seven *hundred* dollars."

"Right—and look at that first name," Jamal added.

"I've never heard of anyone called Iam," Gaby said.

"Hey! It said W. Yafa by Mr. Yafa's doorbell," Jamal said.

"Wiam?" Hector suggested, "That's a funny name."

"I bet it's *Will*iam," Jamal said. He filled in the name in the casebook.

"Maybe Ghostwriter was in a hurry and left off some of the letters," Casey guessed.

"No way," Hector said. "That's not like Ghostwriter. He always brings us the most complete message he can. I think the letters are missing because part of the bill is missing. I bet somebody tore up that water bill after Mr. Yafa paid it."

"The City of New York wouldn't tear up a paid bill. They'd put it in a file to show it was paid," Alex said.

"Yeah," Hector added, "and they'd probably let Mr. Yafa keep a copy, too. Let's try one more thing to make sure."

Hector borrowed the casebook from Jamal and wrote a note to Ghostwriter on a blank page, asking Ghostwriter to read what was around Mr. Yafa's water bill. In a few minutes, Ghostwriter wrote:

The Blaster
ERA 3.50
HAIR: Brown
EYES: Brown

"That looks like stuff on a baseball card," Casey said, "not a water bill. What does that mean?"

"I think I know where Hector's going with this,"

Jamal said thoughtfully. "If the City collected money from a bill, they'd put it in a file with other paid bills, not with baseball cards."

"Exactly," Hector said. Jamal copied Ghostwriter's latest message into the part of the casebook titled "Other Clues."

"Now what?" asked Tina. "I don't see how we're going to find this bill—or the con artist—with the clues we have."

Just then the letters on the casebook started to swirl. It was Ghostwriter with another message: June 13th—Morning—Conrad is still mad at me. I didn't lose the list on purpose. I have to figure out how to find it. This is hard without any friends.

"It seems like the same kid we got that other message from," said Tina. "And it's dated again, like a diary. What should we do?"

"Let's ask Ghostwriter who it is," said Jamal, starting to write on a blank page. Seconds later, Ghostwriter answered: It sounds like someone who needs your help.

"It seems like we have two mysteries to solve here," said Lenni. "First, who ripped off Mr. Yafa? Second, who's writing these messages, and how can we help? Let's start a new page in the casebook and call it 'Mystery Kid.' Then we can keep track of these messages and try to figure them out."

"Good idea," said Jamal, and wrote down both messages. By then it was time for Alex and Gaby to get back to their parents' bodega, the store where they helped out. Hector was anxious to start selling Jumbo Bars to the people on Mr. Yafa's list.

"This is going to be my best sales day yet!" he told the team as they went their separate ways.

But when Hector passed Keisha's table at the supermarket, she was making change for a woman who had just bought two Jumbo Bars. Keisha had put up a sign with a picture of herself in a pink leotard. HELP ME GET TO GYMNASTICS CAMP, it said under the picture.

"Good luck, dear," said the lady as she put the chocolate into her cart.

"Thank you so much, ma'am," said Keisha sweetly. As the lady walked off, Keisha stuck her tongue out at Hector and silently mouthed, *"Ha ha!"*

Earlier that day Keisha's behavior would have made Hector mad, but now he just grinned at her and waved. Then, to rub it in, he unwrapped an almond bar from his bag and took a big bite.

"At least I don't have to worry about eating up my profits," Keisha called out. "I'm allergic to chocolate."

"True, but with the customer list I have now, I can afford to eat some of my profits," said Hector. He took another big bite of chocolate.

"What list? What are you talking about?" Keisha demanded.

"Mmm. Good chocolate," Hector said and strolled away, leaving Keisha staring after him with her mouth hanging open.

Chapter 3

Double Trouble

Before going to the first person on Mr. Yafa's list, Hector stopped to visit his friend Mrs. Astor. She owned a little shop filled with things Hector never got tired of looking at—books and magazines, stamps, stickers, old bowling shirts, army canteens, and a big collection of comic books and trading cards.

Hector had gotten to know Mrs. Astor by spending hours browsing in her store. He thought she was a little strange—she wore odd clothes, as if she were in an old movie or something. But she was a lot of fun, too. She knew tons of sports trivia.

Lately Hector had been visiting her every day because she always bought at least one peanut butter Jumbo Bar.

When Hector got to the shop, Mrs. Astor was sitting in her usual spot by the door, doing word-search puzzles. She wore her favorite blue-and-orange Mets baseball cap, and around her neck were about ten chains and strings of beads—one with a big metal peace symbol.

"Hello, Hector. How's business?" Mrs. Astor's voice sounded like the stars in the old black-and-white movies Hector sometimes saw on TV. It was husky and full, and Mrs. Astor pronounced every word clearly. She loved to tell Hector about her days as an actress. She had even been on Broadway once.

She seemed happy to see Hector, and even happier that he'd brought along several peanut butter bars. Mrs. Astor loved chocolate, but she loved chocolate and peanut butter to death!

As soon as she paid for the candy, she unwrapped it. "I'll just have one small bite," she said to Hector. While they talked, one bite turned into two, which turned into half a bar, and then into the whole bar. Then Mrs. Astor bought another, to keep for later. Then she thought maybe she'd take *one* bite of that bar, which made Hector grin.

"Business is not so good here lately," she said, looking around the empty store. "But this is for a good cause, Hector—your swimming career."

¡Que suerte!—What luck! Hector thought and grinned again. "I've only got two peanut butter bars left, Mrs. Astor, why don't you take them both? You can freeze them so they'll stay fresh." He held the two big candy bars right under her nose.

Mrs. Astor smiled back and gave him two dollars. She pulled another Mets cap from a shelf and plunked it on the boy's head. "You have spirit, Hector. I like doing business with a winner."

Hector told Mrs. Astor about his idea to sell Jumbo Bars door-to-door, and he showed her the list Mr. Yafa had given him. "Do you know Mr. Yafa?"

"No," Mrs. Astor answered.

"Well, he's this really nice old guy—my mother did some work for him—but anyhow, he was very upset today when Jamal and I saw him. He said someone came to collect a huge water bill and he had to give her all his money right on the spot."

"Gracious!" Mrs. Astor declared.

Just then the door slammed and a kid walked in and headed over to the trading cards.

"Jamal and I said we could help Mr. Yafa find out who was behind his water bill and the one his friend Mrs. Washington got," Hector continued. "Mr. Yafa was so grateful, he gave me this list of his friends from the Lunch Bunch. He said they'd be glad to buy candy bars from me."

"You are a clever kid. If you weren't out of peanut butter, I'd buy another bar," Mrs. Astor said. "So how do you plan to help Mr. Yafa?"

"Well, my friends and I are pretty good at solving mysteries. We're going to start by—"

Suddenly something fell on the floor behind Hector. He realized that the kid who had come into the store earlier was close by. He had the feeling the kid had been listening to his conversation with Mrs. Astor.

"Who's that?" Hector asked, trying to see the kid's face as the kid walked to the front of the store and out the door.

"Some kid who's been spending a lot of time here," Mrs. Astor said. "The kid's crazy about base-ball cards—looks at 'em all day, but doesn't seem to have the money to buy too many."

Hector shrugged and headed toward the door himself.

"What was Gregg Jefferies' 1991 batting average?" Mrs. Astor quizzed him. She always asked one sports question before Hector left the store. When Hector hesitated, she had the answer right on the tip of her tongue. "Two seventy-two." She laughed. "I'm always right about the Mets, right?"

"Yeah," Hector replied with a grin. "So long!"

As Hector left, he saw the kid who had been in the store turning the corner. Suddenly Hector noticed letters flying up in the air. It seemed as if they were coming out of the kid's backpack. The cloud of letters came together on a big advertising billboard across the street.

June 13th—Afternoon—I wonder why Mrs. Washington and Mr. Yafa and Mrs. Zuni were so sad today. Is it my fault? Will Mrs. Vega be next?

Hector scribbled the message down on one of his order cards. *It seems like another diary entry from the mystery kid,* he thought. Hector wondered how the mystery kid knew his friend, Mr. Yafa. He tucked the note in his pocket. He would show it to the team later.

He hurried off to see the first person on Mr. Yafa's list. Mrs. Alvarez lived just around the corner. On his way there, Hector had the feeling someone was following him. He looked over his shoulder and thought he saw a kid in a blue-and-orange baseball cap. *Maybe it's Keisha following me, trying to mess up my sales,* Hector thought. *Then again, maybe it's that kid from Mrs. Astor's store.*

Hector started walking faster. He heard the footsteps behind him speed up, too. Then he slowed down, and the footsteps slowed. Hector started to sweat. *Is someone going to mug me?* he wondered.

Hector broke into a run. He heard footsteps pounding right behind him. He clenched his teeth and ran as hard as he could, dodging the people on the sidewalk. Some turned and glared at him as he charged by. But after a block, Hector noticed that the footsteps behind him had stopped. He slowed down and looked back. Whoever was after him was gone—at least for now.

Hector walked slowly until his heartbeat quieted down enough for him to think. He remembered he had been on his way to Mrs. Alvarez's building, and decided to go there.

When he arrived, Mrs. Alvarez answered the door right away. She was a thin woman with lots of energy. In the middle of her living room there was a large wooden frame with a colorful strip of fabric on it. She explained to Hector that she was weaving a rug, and she showed him how she threw the shuttle full of red wool back and forth, making the rug longer. Hector watched politely for a few minutes.

"Mrs. Alvarez," he finally said, "I'm hoping you will buy a candy bar from me today." He unrolled his poster listing five reasons to buy a Jumbo Bar.

The poster made Mrs. Alvarez laugh. "I don't eat much chocolate myself," she said. "But I guess I could use two bars for when I have visitors. Do you have almond?" She handed him two dollars.

Hector didn't even have to make change. *This is going to work out great!* he thought.

The next two people on his list lived in Mrs. Alvarez's building. Mr. Bowen was right next door, so Hector stopped there first. There was no one home, so Hector hung his calling card on the doorknob. He did the same thing at Mrs. Cisneros' apartment upstairs.

Hector scanned the list and realized that the next dozen people on it lived several blocks away. He looked at the bottom of the list. The fourth person from the end—Mrs. Vega—lived just down the street in Mr. Yafa's building. So did the last person on the list, Mrs. Zuni. Hector decided to head there.

Hector had to ring Mrs. Vega's bell a few times before she answered. As soon as he began his sales pitch, Mrs. Vega tried to send him away.

"Not today," she said. "Not for a long time. I just paid a man from the City a water bill big enough to buy Niagara Falls. It took all my money for the month, over four hundred and fifty dollars.

"It's a good thing I get food from the Lunch Bunch," she added softly. "That's all I'm going to have in my fridge for the next three weeks."

Hector asked Mrs. Vega to describe the man. "To be honest, I was so upset I didn't get a good look at him. I think he was slender. He wore a big hat, a sort of beret, and he had a strange French accent and a high voice," Mrs. Vega said. She was too upset to remember anything else.

Hector felt so sorry for Mrs. Vega, he almost offered her a free Jumbo Bar. Instead he wrote down what she had said.

"I'll be all right," Mrs. Vega said. Then she closed her door.

Hector walked down one flight and knocked on Mrs. Zuni's door. After a minute he heard shuffling footsteps, and then a bolt being pulled back. When the door opened, Hector only needed to take one look at Mrs. Zuni's face to see that she had been crying. A few quick questions confirmed his fears— Mrs. Zuni had also gotten a water bill! *This is too weird,* thought Hector.

It was time to call the police. He headed to the bodega, where Alex and Gaby were working. On his way, he got the feeling he was being followed again. He spun around, but in the crowd of people, he couldn't tell who was following him. *Maybe the stress of trying to be a top chocolate salesman is making me imagine things,* Hector thought. But he couldn't shake the feeling he was being tailed.

He started to jog down the sidewalk, past stores

and apartment buildings. That's when he knew someone *was* after him. He could hear footsteps following him, and someone panting. He started to run and heard a voice shout, "Hey, come back! *Stop!*" Hector ran faster. Then the strangest thing happened. Instead of getting *away* from the footsteps, Hector heard *more* footsteps—it sounded as if a whole gang was after him.

He looked over his shoulder and saw three teenagers—big ones—coming after him. "Yo! Stop! Didn't you hear the kid say stop?" they yelled.

Hector thought he must be losing his mind. *What did I ever do to these guys? Why are they after me?*

The next thing Hector knew, someone grabbed him around the waist and threw him onto the pavement. He was pinned to the sidewalk on his stomach. One guy was twisting his right arm behind his back, and it hurt.

"What did you steal?" a big, mean-looking boy shouted at him. "You took that kid's wallet, right? Where is it?"

"I didn't steal anything. Let me go!" Hector cried.

"Then what was the kid after you for?"

"I don't know. I never saw that kid in my life. You can search me if you want. I don't have anyone's wallet."

Something about Hector's face must have convinced them.

"Okay. Let him go." The three walked away as if nothing had happened. Hector got up and brushed himself off. His arm was sore and he was shaken up, but otherwise he was okay.

He cut through an empty lot and onto another sidewalk, and finally got to Alex and Gaby's bodega. He was relieved to see his friends. He told them all about being chased—twice—which made him feel a little better.

Then he remembered the message he'd gotten from Ghostwriter as he left Mrs. Astor's store. He read it to them: "'June 13th—Afternoon—I wonder why Mrs. Washington and Mr. Yafa and Mrs. Zuni were so sad today. Is it my fault? Will Mrs. Vega be next?'"

"It says, 'Will Mrs. Vega be next?'" Hector repeated. "Well, guess what? She *was* next! I went to her apartment to sell her a Jumbo Bar and she had just paid a big water bill. Then I went to Mrs. Zuni's and she had just paid a water bill for more than four hundred and fifty dollars!" Hector quickly filled the team in on the description Mrs. Zuni had given him of her bill collector. She said the bill collector was a woman with some kind of accent, wearing black, baggy clothes.

"So we know for sure the people giving out fake bills have hit at least four people already: Mr. Yafa, Mrs. Vega, Mrs. Washington, and Mrs. Zuni, right?" said Gaby.

"I think we should try calling Lieutenant McQuade about this," said Hector. "It's getting serious."

"I'll do it," said Alex, picking up the phone.

When Alex hung up a few minutes later, the thirteen-year-old did not look happy. "The officer who answered said Lieutenant McQuade is out sick. I kept telling him we've helped Lieutenant McQuade in the past, but he didn't seem to be taking me seriously. I bet he thinks we're kids playing pranks."

"Well, let's keep working on this," Gaby said, pointing to the message from the mystery kid.

June 13th—Afternoon—I wonder why Mrs. Washington and Mr. Yafa and Mrs. Zuni were so sad today. Is it my fault? Will Mrs. Vega be next?

"The kid wonders if it's his or her fault that these people were so sad. And we know that all four of these people got fake water bills. Does that mean the kid had something to do with the water bills?"

"Maybe so," said Hector. He quickly wrote a question to Ghostwriter: "What does the mystery kid have to do with fake water bills?"

Ghostwriter's glow swooped over Hector's question, then cleared away all the letters except for a big, black **?**

"Jamal's got the casebook," said Hector. "But I'll keep this message so we can copy it into the casebook." As Hector stuck the note into his backpack, he saw a folded piece of paper that hadn't been there before. He opened it and his face went pale.

"What's the matter?" Alex asked.

"Look at this. Someone put this message right in my backpack."

Hector read the note to Alex and Gaby. It said:

Are you trying to help Mr. Yafa? Find out about Mrs. Vega. I think Mr. Underhill could be next.

"This must have been put here when I was being tailed today," said Hector shakily. "But what does it mean? Is it a help or a threat?"

Suddenly Ghostwriter's glow swirled over the note. A new message appeared. It said: From Mystery Kid.

"*Wow!*" said Alex. "It's from the kid whose diary we read, only now he's writing straight to us!"

"We need to put this in our 'Mystery Kid' list in the casebook," said Gaby. "Can you rally tomorrow at noon?"

"Sure," Hector answered. Gaby wrote a message for the rest of the team. The letters trailed out like a flag as Ghostwriter carried the message to them: RALLY, Fort Greene Park. Tomorrow 12 noon.

Chapter 4

On the Case

The next day the team met in the park near a statue of Civil War heroes. "I like this spot. There's lots of open space and we can see if anyone's spying on us," said Hector. "That note I got gave me the creeps. Somebody had to be following me to slip that note into my backpack. What if the person is still following me?"

Alex, Gaby, and Hector filled the others in on what had happened the day before. Jamal handed Hector the casebook so that he could copy the newest information.

Then Hector told the team what had happened that morning. "I went back to two apartments where I had left my cards—Mr. Bowen's and Mrs. Cisneros'. Mr. Bowen wasn't home. But Mrs. Cisneros told me to go away. She wouldn't even open her door. She said she was completely broke after paying a big bill and the last thing she needed to do was spend money on chocolate! I asked if it was a water bill and she wouldn't answer."

Then Hector explained that he had left cards on the doors of three more people on his list: Mrs. Dowling, Mrs. Eisen, and Mr. Fugard. "I sure hope these bogus water bill collectors don't hit them before I can get back this afternoon," he said. "Or the world may be robbed of a great Olympic star named Hector Carrero."

"It's Sunday," Gaby pointed out as she swirled her curly ponytail around one finger. "Bill collectors don't work on Sunday."

"*Real* bill collectors don't work on Sunday," Jamal corrected her. "If people get hit with bills today, that will be more evidence that the whole thing is a trick."

"I don't get it," Hector complained. "Why does everybody on my Lunch Bunch list get a water bill?"

"We don't know that it's *only* people on your list. But let's look at the evidence in the casebook again," said Lenni.

Under "Evidence" it said:

BOGUS BILLS COLLECTED FROM:
Mr. Yafa
Mrs. Washington
Mrs. Vega
Mrs. Zuni
Mrs. Cisneros

Casey picked up the casebook. She looked at the messages from the mystery kid. Then she copied down the names of people in the kid's note. She added those names to the list of names under "Evidence" in a new order:

Mrs. Cisneros
Mr. Underhill
Mrs. Vega
Mrs. Washington
Mr. Yafa
Mrs. Zuni

 Attention, Reader:

Can you see what Casey has noticed about the names of the people who got water bills? Hint: It has something to do with the order of the names.

—Ghostwriter

Casey jumped up and shook the casebook at the others. "I've got it!"

"What?" Jamal asked.

Casey read the new list: "Mrs. Cisneros, Mr. Underhill, Mrs. Vega, Mrs. Washington, Mr. Yafa, and Mrs. Zuni! Drop Mrs. Cisneros' name, and then look at the first letters of all of the names that are left: *U, V, W, Y, Z!*"

"Hey, the names are in alphabetical order!" Lenni said.

"And look at this!" Hector was shouting, he was so excited. "Those names are on my Lunch Bunch list—in the *same* order!"

"So that means the con artists *might* be using the Lunch Bunch list," Lenni added.

"But those names all start with letters at the end of the alphabet. The con artist must have started at the end of the Lunch Bunch list and worked backward," Jamal pointed out.

"But wait a minute," Hector said. "Yesterday afternoon the bill collector went to see Mrs. Cisneros. Her name starts with *C*."

"But she's also on your Lunch Bunch list, right?" Lenni asked.

"Yeah. Near the *beginning* of my list. Maybe the bill collectors switched to the beginning of the list," Hector said. Suddenly his eyes grew wide. "What about Mrs. Alvarez? She hadn't gotten a bill when I saw her yesterday. Now I'm worried about her. And

Mr. Bowen's also before Mrs. Cisneros on the list. I wonder if he's been given a bill?"

"Let's go and find out if they got bills," Casey said, jumping up and grabbing Hector's hand to pull him up, too. They both headed out of the park.

Lenni, Alex, and Jamal decided they would interview the people who had already been hit with bills to see if they could remember anything more about the bill collectors. "And let's hang up some signs in these buildings to warn people about what's going on," said Jamal.

Tina and Gaby said they'd call the police station to see if anyone had reported strange water bills.

Everyone agreed to meet in two hours.

As they were leaving, Lenni grabbed Alex's elbow and pointed behind the monument. "Something moved," she whispered. "Over there."

"Where?" asked Alex.

"Right near the two soldiers on the left side of the monument. I think I saw someone move."

"Oh boy, Lenni," said Jamal. "You're starting to see things."

Jamal stopped talking. "Wait a minute. I think I saw someone, too," he whispered. "Let's check it out."

Lenni, Jamal, and Alex started creeping toward the monument, trying not to make any noise. As they got near the left side, Lenni shrieked. A kid with a backpack and a blue-and-orange cap jumped down from the monument, nearly knocking Lenni over, and ran out of the park.

"How could that kid have known about the rally?" Gaby wondered aloud. "Maybe that's the kid who left the note in Hector's backpack yesterday—and followed him here this morning."

Mrs. Alvarez was like a different person when she answered Hector and Casey's knock. The energy had gone out of her like air seeping out of an old balloon. She did not seem glad to see them. She barely opened the door, and she said she couldn't ask them in; she told them she had the flu. The whole time she was talking, she kept looking up and down the hall, as if she was watching for someone.

"What are you afraid of, Mrs. Alvarez?" Casey asked. "Maybe we can help you."

Mrs. Alvarez didn't say anything for a minute. She looked hard at Hector and Casey, and then she invited them inside. They had barely sat down at her kitchen table before the words began pouring out of Mrs. Alvarez's mouth.

"I talked to Mr. Bowen in the hall today, and he said not to open my door to anyone."

"Well, we're glad you let *us* in," Hector said. He helped himself to one of the oatmeal cookies Mrs. Alvarez put out on a plate. "Can you tell us exactly what happened?"

"I was doing the dishes after supper yesterday and watching *Star Trek: The Next Generation* on the little TV I keep on the shelf above the sink. The doorbell rang, and I thought it was my granddaughter. She usually stops by on Saturday night, so I just buzzed her into the building, unlocked the door to my apartment, and went right back to the program."

While Mrs. Alvarez was talking, she poured glasses of milk for Hector and Casey. It looked as if some of her old spirit was coming back.

"All of a sudden, I turned around and there was this . . . *person* . . . standing in the doorway. I had never seen her before in my life!"

Casey made notes as Mrs. Alvarez talked. Hector asked her to describe the person, and Mrs. Alvarez frowned as if she were having trouble remembering.

"She was wearing a funny kind of a soft hat and a big sweater, so you couldn't see what color her hair was or if she was fat or thin. The hallway light was burned out, so her face was in the shadows. She talked in a funny high voice with an accent—maybe Spanish, but it was hard to tell because she kept coughing.

"Then she dangled this bill in front of me and insisted I pay over four hundred dollars! I don't have cash like that around. All I had was fifty dollars, so I asked her to come in so we could talk things over. I said maybe we could even call someone at the City office and work out a way to pay the bill bit by bit."

Casey looked up from her notes and asked, "What did she do about that?"

"She wouldn't come in. She said she was busy enough as it was. She said she'd take my fifty dollars and come back today for the rest. Well, now it's today, and I don't have any more money! I don't know what I'm going to do when she comes." Hector thought Mrs. Alvarez looked as if she was going to cry. "That's all I can tell you," she said.

"It's plenty," Casey said, writing fast to keep up with Mrs. Alvarez's story.

"Can you remember anything else about how she looked?" Hector asked. "If we can find this bill collector, maybe we can figure out what's going on."

"The voice is the main thing I remember," Mrs. Alvarez said. "It was so strange and squeaky."

Hector thanked Mrs. Alvarez for all her help and promised to keep her posted. "In the meantime," he cautioned her, "if that woman comes back today, don't give her anything. We think this whole thing might be some kind of con game."

Mrs. Alvarez said she felt much better knowing that somebody was following up on the case and that she was glad she could help a little. She stuffed the last few cookies into Casey's pocket and told the kids to call if she could help any further.

After they left Mrs. Alvarez, Hector suggested

they stop by the other apartments where he had left his cards: Mr. Bowen's, Mrs. Dowling's, Mrs. Eisen's, and Mr. Fugard's. There was no answer at Mr. Bowen's or Mrs. Dowling's, and nobody came to the door at Mrs. Eisen's, even though Casey and Hector could hear a TV through the door. But when they got to Mr. Fugard's apartment, the kids were in for a big shock.

Hector didn't think he'd ever seen anybody as mad as Mr. Fugard. With every word he spoke, he seemed to grow taller and redder and more furious. Casey and Hector didn't try to reason with him. They got out of there, fast!

"I bet the con artist hit Mr. Fugard, too," Casey said once they were far enough from the building to be sure he hadn't followed them. Hector took another look at his Lunch Bunch list and put check marks beside the names of all the people who had gotten bills: Mrs. Zuni, Mrs. Washington, Mr. Yafa, Mrs. Vega—then Mrs. Alvarez, Mrs. Cisneros, and Mr. Fugard.

"We don't know for sure about Mr. Bowen, Mrs. Dowling, or Mrs. Eisen, but it's pretty likely they've been hit, too," Hector said. "I wish we had the phone numbers of everyone on this list so we could call them up and warn them."

"Yeah," Casey said. "I'm kind of scared to ring any more of those doorbells."

Hector said he was going to stop and see if Mrs. Astor's store was open so that he could sell at least one Jumbo Bar. Casey headed back to the park to meet the rest of the team.

When Hector walked into the store, Mrs. Astor was perched on a stool in the back going through her scrapbook. Her armful of bangle bracelets jingled as she turned each page. A bunch of kids were in the front, looking at trading cards and comic books.

Mrs. Astor smiled when she saw Hector. She waved him over to look at the scrapbook. It was full of photographs of a much younger Mrs. Astor, when she was an actress. It also had yellowing newspaper articles about the plays in which she'd appeared.

"I had such a promising career," Mrs. Astor said with a faraway look in her eyes. "I never could figure out what went wrong."

After a couple of seconds, she smiled at Hector and started nibbling on a fresh peanut butter Jumbo Bar. "But if I were still on the stage, I wouldn't be here eating this delicious candy bar and talking to one of my favorite kids." She patted Hector's arm and reached into the pocket of her skirt for some money.

While Mrs. Astor looked for her money, Hector glanced at the kids looking through the trading cards and comic books. He saw the kid he'd seen in the store the day before. The kid was wearing a blue-and-orange Mets cap and looking through the baseball section of the trading cards.

"Hey," Hector called, and started toward the display racks. Quick as a wink, the kid spun around and ran out of the store. Then Ghostwriter's glow came whirling in, and Ghostwriter pulled letters off some baseball cards. A message sparkled in the air above the rack: Look at *Hoodman Saves the 'Hood.*

Trying to look casual, Hector strolled over to the comic books and found the issue of *Hoodman.* When Hector opened the comic book, a page that looked as if it had been torn from a notebook dropped on the floor. It said: "I must find the lost list."

Back in the park later that day, Hector showed the team the message that had fallen out of the comic book. Jamal copied it into the casebook. "This was left for me on purpose," Hector said, "but I don't know how that kid would know to find me in Mrs. Astor's."

"Lenni and I think we saw the kid in the park at noontime, right after you left," Alex said. "Maybe you were being followed."

"Was he wearing a Mets cap?" Hector asked.

"Yes," Lenni said, "but we couldn't tell if it was a girl or a boy."

"I bet that was the same kid I've seen twice in

Mrs. Astor's! I couldn't tell if it was a boy or a girl either," Hector said. "But if that's the kid whose diary we've read and who left the note in my backpack, then that was our mystery kid."

"So somehow the mystery kid has started following us," Jamal said.

"Rewind!" Casey sang out. "Can we take another look at all the evidence?"

"Okay," Alex said. "We know the list the kid is talking about has a lot of the same names as the Lunch Bunch list, right?"

"Probably," Jamal said, always careful not to jump to conclusions. "Let's look at all the messages again."

MYSTERY KID
I'm in BIG trouble now.

June 12th—Conrad got so mad at me for losing it. I wish I had someone to talk to about this. I'm so far away from home. I'm scared.

June 13th—Morning—Conrad is still mad at me. I didn't lose the list on purpose. I have to figure out how to find it. This is hard without any friends.

June 13th—Afternoon—I wonder why Mrs. Washington and Mr. Yafa and Mrs. Zuni were

so sad today. Is it my fault? Will Mrs. Vega
be next?

NOTE IN HECTOR'S BACKPACK
Are you trying to help Mr. Yafa? Find out about
Mrs. Vega. I think Mr. Underhill could be next.

NOTE THAT FELL FROM COMIC BOOK
I must find the lost list. (Same handwriting as
note in Hector's backpack.)

"We *think* the con artists are using the Lunch
Bunch list to rip off those old people," Lenni insisted. Everyone agreed.

"How would con artists get the Lunch Bunch list?
Who would have this list?" asked Alex.

"If we could answer those questions, we'd have
some possible suspects," said Gaby.

"Well, who runs the Lunch Bunch program?"
asked Alex.

"I know," said Gaby. "I used to volunteer at the
Community Center. A guy named Mr. Steiner drives
the Lunch Bunch van. He used to teach the acting
classes there, too, and he works in a theater. I just
can't think of his first name."

"Hey!" Hector said. "I know another person who
had a way to get the list. Keisha! She used to do volunteer work for the Lunch Bunch, so she might have
the list."

"But she's a kid," Gaby said. "Nobody said the bill collectors were kids."

Hector refused to be discouraged. "She could be the lookout. She could case the street for cops while she's pretending to sell Jumbo Bars."

"All right," Jamal said, writing Keisha down as a suspect. "I guess if any kid did that, Keisha would."

Suddenly Gaby gasped. "Conrad. It's Conrad!"

"Gaby, what are you talking about?" Alex asked.

"I remembered the first name of the Lunch Bunch driver. It's Conrad. And that's the name the mystery kid mentioned in his diary!"

"She's right," said Jamal, looking at the casebook. "The kid wrote: 'Conrad got so mad at me for losing it.'"

"Maybe the kid is working with Conrad," Tina suggested.

Jamal opened the casebook to the suspect list. It looked like this:

SUSPECT—MR. YAFA'S BILL COLLECTOR

Woman
Brownish hair
Big sweater
Southern accent

EVIDENCE
Collected over $700 from Mr. Yafa

SUSPECT—MRS. WASHINGTON'S BILL
COLLECTOR
Man
German accent

EVIDENCE
Collected $430 from Mrs. Washington

SUSPECT—MRS. VEGA'S BILL
COLLECTOR
Man
Slender
Wore a big beret-style hat
Strange French accent and high voice

EVIDENCE
Collected over $450 from Mrs. Vega

SUSPECT—MRS. ZUNI'S BILL COLLECTOR
Woman
Black, baggy clothes
Some kind of accent

EVIDENCE
Collected more than $450 from Mrs. Zuni

SUSPECT—MRS. ALVAREZ'S BILL
COLLECTOR
Woman
Funny soft hat
Big sweater
Coughed a lot
Squeaky, high voice with accent—maybe
Spanish

EVIDENCE
Collected $50 from Mrs. Alvarez

At the bottom of the page he added:

SUSPECT
Keisha

EVIDENCE
Was volunteer at Lunch Bunch so could have
list

SUSPECT
Conrad, the Lunch Bunch van driver

EVIDENCE
He has the Lunch Bunch list
The mystery kid mentioned him

"The Lunch Bunch van driver has an assistant, a

kid who volunteers," said Gaby. "Whoever that is, he or she should go on the suspect list, too."

So Jamal wrote:

SUSPECT
Assistant X

EVIDENCE
Works on van so has Lunch Bunch list

But nothing else seemed clear. Lenni, Alex, and Jamal had talked to the latest victims earlier that day, and every person had given a different description of the water bill collector. According to Mrs. Washington, it was a man with a German accent. Mrs. Zuni said it was a woman with an accent she'd never heard before, and Mr. Underhill said it was a very small man who talked so softly Mr. Underhill could barely hear him.

"Wow," said Casey. "Maybe there's a whole gang of water bill collectors and they have the same list Hector has. They go where he goes."

"Maybe it would help if we got another copy of one of the water bills," Gaby suggested. "It might be in better condition than Mr. Yafa's bill was, or there might be another clue on it."

The team asked Ghostwriter to find them a City of New York water bill. In a flash his message came back:

```
City of New York
Brooklyn
Water Bill

Dr. Alice Graves......................$402.75
```

"That's a new name," Lenni remarked.

"It's the next one on my list, after Mr. Fugard," Hector added, checking his paper.

"The bill doesn't say 'paid,'" Tina pointed out. "Maybe it hasn't been delivered yet."

Suddenly Gaby put a finger to her lips. "Shhh—look over there," she said and pointed to some woods nearby.

"What?" Casey got scared and grabbed Lenni's hand.

"I thought for a minute somebody was spying on us from over there in those trees," said Gaby. "Jamal, come check it out with me."

Gaby and Jamal jogged over to the edge of the woods and looked for signs of movement. Everything seemed perfectly still, except for leaves rustling in the light breeze.

Something caught Gaby's eye, and she poked Jamal and pointed straight into the woods. They saw something bright blue moving. The next thing they knew, someone was crashing through the woods, deeper into the forest, running away from them.

"Come on," said Jamal, grabbing Gaby's hand. "I know this part of the park. We'll run along the edge of the woods to the other side. I bet they're going to come out of the woods there."

As Jamal and Gaby circled around the woods, they could hear someone running through the underbrush. Just as they got within sight of the place where Jamal thought the person would exit, a kid came sprinting out of the woods, heading straight for the park exit.

"Gaby, run!" shouted Jamal, and the two took off, trying to catch the kid. They started closing in, but not in time. The kid made it out of the park and jumped into a van that was parked near the exit.

Gaby tried to get a good look at the driver as the van took off. She was shocked. "That looks exactly like Conrad," she told Jamal.

"This is too weird," was all Jamal could say as they headed back to the rest of the team.

"We missed him—or her," Gaby told the team. "But here's what's really weird. It looked like the kid got into a van driven by Conrad!"

"Maybe the two of them are a team—they're conning people, and now they're spying on us since we're working on this case," said Casey.

"It's possible," said Jamal. "But we need more evidence. And right now it's time to get home for dinner." He picked up the casebook and handed it to

Hector. "I've got karate tomorrow morning. Why don't you stake out Dr. Graves' apartment and see if you can catch one of the con artists in the act?"

"Okay," said Hector. "Alex, Gaby, Casey, and I can go there tomorrow. If she hasn't been hit by one of the con artists yet, maybe she'll buy a few candy bars from a kid with a great attitude." He sounded glum.

Hector waved to his friends and walked around the Civil War statue. His eye was caught by a baseball card lying on the ground. It was the card for Gregg Jefferies, the player Mrs. Astor had quizzed him about! Hector picked it up and saw a note stuck to the back. It was in the same handwriting as the note the mystery kid had left in Hector's backpack and the note that fell out of the comic book. It said:

I don't think it's Conrad! If I can just remember where I lost the list, I can help solve this. Don't give up!

Chapter 5

Stakeout

Hector didn't sleep well. All night he kept having nightmares about chocolate. He dreamed that his mother served an all-chocolate dinner: chocolate bars, chocolate ice cream, chocolate milk. "Come on, Hector, eat it all or you can't go to swimming camp," scolded his mother. He woke up in a cold sweat. Now, as he watched the sunlight coming through the window, he felt hopeless. He didn't see how he could ever catch up with Keisha.

Hector thought maybe he was having nightmares because he was so involved with the water bill case that he wasn't selling much chocolate. One thing he was sure about was that Keisha was a strong suspect. Maybe she was helping to give out the fake water bills so that Hector couldn't sell any of those people chocolate. She was big for her age, and could easily be part of the gang of con artists.

Suddenly Hector remembered that the stakeout at Dr. Graves' apartment was today. He jumped out of bed and pulled on his jeans and a T-shirt. For good luck, he wore the Mets cap Mrs. Astor had given him.

"Good morning, *hijo*," his mother called as he walked into the kitchen. "You've been working so hard to sell your chocolate, I made you one of your favorite breakfasts—waffles. You can even dribble on a little chocolate sauce if you want."

Hector gulped. "Ah, no thanks, Mama. I'll just have regular syrup."

On the way to Dr. Graves' house, Hector passed Keisha, already busy at her table selling Jumbo Bars. He still had a little time before he had to meet the others, and he thought he might collect some evidence. He walked up to Keisha.

"Excuse me, Keisha," he said.

"Yeeessss," Keisha replied, narrowing her eyes suspiciously.

"Well, I—I just wanted to say you were totally right when you said that selling candy door-to-door was a terrible idea. And I thought maybe later today, when you're done selling, or if you take a little break . . . maybe you'd let me use your table for a while."

"That's very funny, Mr. Big Salesman. Ha-ha-ha. Would Coke help Pepsi? Would Ford help Chevy? Would Big Bird help Mickey Mouse?"

"Yeah, Keisha, I think Big Bird might help Mickey—"

"Well, I'm not going to help *you*!" Keisha said. She smiled wickedly. "Have a nice day."

Hector shook his head and was about to leave when he saw a stack of fliers on the table. "What're those?" he asked.

"Publicity. I put them in front of some of the apartments around here."

"Which apartments?"

Keisha smiled smugly. "That's for me to know and you to find out."

"Well, I'll just check it out, if you don't mind." He snatched a flier before Keisha could object. *Wow!* Hector thought as he hurried to the stakeout. *This flier could be a piece of evidence. Maybe Keisha marks apartments for the con artist by putting fliers there.* He opened the casebook to Keisha's page and wrote "fliers" under the "Evidence" section. He tucked the flier in to read later.

As Hector approached the building where Dr. Graves lived, he saw the Lunch Bunch van parked in front. Then he saw a man who he figured must be Conrad open the back door of the van, take out a package, and dart into the building. *What could he be up to?* Hector wondered.

He could hardly wait to tell the team about the new evidence he had, and he ran for the elevator. The doors were just closing as he got there—and Conrad was inside! *Rats,* Hector thought, and he ran for the stairs.

At each floor, Hector looked down the hall to see if Conrad was there. Then he ran up another flight. He was gasping for breath when he got to the fifth floor and saw Conrad.

The slender man was already at the door of one of the apartments, and he was speaking very softly to the woman inside. Hector couldn't hear what they were saying, but it looked as if the woman was crying. Conrad turned to go. The old woman watched him walk back to the elevator, blew her nose on a big handkerchief, and then shut the door.

Hector forgot he was out of breath. He raced up two more flights of stairs to the stakeout on the seventh floor. Alex, Casey, and Gaby were already waiting in the stairwell, where they could watch Dr. Graves' apartment without being spotted. Hector quickly told them what he had seen. "Maybe Conrad is the leader of the gang." Then he pulled Keisha's flier from the casebook. "This might be more evidence against Keisha. Maybe she marks the doors for the con artists."

"If Conrad's in this building, some of us should go interview him," Gaby said. "We'll see if we should keep him on the suspect list."

"I'll go with you," said Alex quickly, with a protective look at his little sister. He and Gaby took off. Hector and Casey sat on the stairs, getting more bored by the minute. Casey thought she heard a noise in the stairway below them, but when Hector listened he didn't hear anything. "You're just so bored you're imagining things," he told Casey.

Hector dumped his Jumbo Bars out of the bag to count how many he had left. He was up to thirteen when Casey grabbed his arm.

"Shh!" she whispered. "There it is again!" The two stayed very still. They didn't hear anything for nearly a minute. Hector was about to let out his breath when they heard footsteps creeping down the stairs below them.

"I bet it was Keisha, trying to listen to my strategy," Hector guessed.

"Or that kid, following you again," Casey said.

Fifteen minutes later, Gaby and Alex came back, out of breath and empty-handed. They had missed Conrad completely.

An hour later, Gaby had worked four crossword puzzles in her book. Casey had read every story and comic she had brought with her. Hector had gone down the hall to see if Mrs. Eisen was home so that he could sell her a candy bar. But no one answered the door.

No con artists had shown up, and everyone was ready to call it a day—everyone but Hector. It was a doubly wasted day for him—no phony bill collectors caught and no candy bars sold!

"Go if you want," he told the team. "I'm at least going to try to see if Dr. Graves will buy some candy."

By the time he rang Dr. Graves' bell, the other team members were gone. She talked to Hector through the door; he knew she was watching him through the peephole. "Is there anyone with you?" she wanted to know.

"No, Dr. Graves, I'm alone. I only wanted to sell you a Jumbo Bar."

"People have been talking about a con artist. How do I know you're really selling Jumbo Bars?"

"My name's Hector Carrero. Call the Community Center. They'll tell you I'm really in the Jumbo Bar contest. And if you buy one, you'll find out how much calmer you feel after you get a little of this soothing chocolate in your system."

Hector smiled and held the bar up temptingly. The doctor snorted a laugh and let the peephole close. *Another lost sale,* Hector thought. *This water bill scam has made my door-to-door sales a total bust.*

Hector walked down the hall, his feet dragging

and his shoulders slumped. He didn't notice that someone was coming toward him until he ran smack into the person. Jumbo Bars flew in all directions. The person who had run into Hector—he thought it was an older woman—turned and walked away without trying to help him collect the candy.

Hector was still picking up Jumbo Bars when he found a piece of paper on the floor. "Hey! You dropped this!" Hector waved the piece of paper, but the person was gone.

Hector shrugged and pressed the Down button for the elevator. In the lobby of the building, he was about to throw the piece of paper away when the writing on it caught his eye: It was a "City of New York Water Bill" made out to Dr. Graves! Hector shook his head in disbelief. The person he ran into must have been the phony bill collector. If only he'd gotten a better look!

Hector whipped out his Ghostwriter pen and wrote a message on his hand: "Rally H." Then he carefully put the bill into his backpack.

He started home, but had taken only a couple of steps before he got the feeling someone was following him. *Not again,* Hector thought. This was too much! When he looked back, he saw a few people, but nobody looked suspicious. Hector turned a corner, but he still had the creepy feeling that someone was on his tail.

Hector suddenly felt himself yanked hard. He couldn't turn, he couldn't get free. This was no mystery kid. It was a grown-up. And the grown-up was pulling him into an abandoned building.

Chapter 6

Kidnapped!

Hector tried to get loose by squirming and kicking, but he was no match for his captor. He started to yell for help, but a handkerchief was stuffed into his mouth. Before he could reach up to grab it away, his hands were yanked back and tied.

Suddenly he was pushed to the ground and rolled up in something that felt like a heavy blanket. He could hardly breathe! Then he was lifted and stuffed into what felt like a shopping cart. Hector couldn't move. When he tried to scream for help, the only thing that came out of his mouth was a muffled squeak.

Then Hector's kidnapper took him for a very bumpy ride. Hector jerked every time the cart went over a curb or a rough patch of sidewalk. At last the cart came to a stop. Hector heard a door being opened on very creaky hinges.

Hector was pushed inside a moldy-smelling place and dumped onto the floor. "Ouch!" mumbled Hector. The kidnapper unrolled the blanket but left Hector blindfolded and gagged. Hector felt his arms being retied behind him so that the ropes were holding his wrists tight against what felt like a wooden column. He couldn't even reach for his pen to send a message to Ghostwriter or the team.

The team! Hector remembered that he had just called a rally. Everyone must be at his apartment by now. Hector wondered if his mom was home. She would be awfully worried about him. Tears welled up in his eyes, and the blindfold soaked them up.

Just as Hector thought, the team was gathered in the hall outside his apartment. Mrs. Carrero wasn't home. And the team couldn't figure out where Hector was. Alex, Gaby, and Casey told the others they hadn't seen him since they'd left him at Dr. Graves' apartment.

"Maybe he got so carried away selling Jumbo Bars that he forgot he called a rally," Tina said.

"Not Hector," Alex said, looking out the window again. "If Hector called a rally, he wouldn't forget about it."

"Well, he's only a little late," Gaby said, sitting down on the floor to wait. Just then letters from Gaby's puzzle book swirled into the air and spelled a message on the wall: I'm in BIG trouble now!

"Who? Who's in trouble? Ask Ghostwriter!" Gaby could hardly write with Jamal and Casey poking at her, but she finally got the question down.

This was Ghostwriter's reply: SUSPECT: Conrad, the Lunch Bunch van driver. EVIDENCE: He has the Lunch Bunch list.

"It's from the casebook!" Jamal and Lenni both got the idea at the same time. "Hector had the casebook last, so Ghostwriter must be where he is!" Jamal wrote as fast as he could: "Where did you find this, Ghostwriter?"

Ghostwriter came back quickly with a reply: 227 Clinton Street.

Gaby recognized the address. It was the building where Dr. Graves lived. It was the last place they had been. "Let's go!" she yelled.

Hector wasn't going anywhere. He was still tied and gagged, his back against the wall. Now, suddenly, a flashlight was shining in his face through the blindfold.

"Where is it?" the kidnapper whispered. The voice

was so low, Hector couldn't tell if it was a man or a woman. "Tell me! You have to give it to me," the kidnapper snarled. Then the person shook Hector, hard. He groaned, and the shaking stopped.

"You stole a piece of paper that belongs to me. Give it back." Hector groaned again. He still had the gag on and he couldn't say anything. "I'll take the gag off," the kidnapper whispered, "But don't try anything funny."

Hector shook his head vigorously. He wanted that gag off. He felt it being pulled away. Hector took a huge gulp of air. Without meaning to, he let out a small sob.

"Where's the paper?" hissed the voice again.

"What paper?"

"Don't play innocent with me," the kidnapper growled.

Hector thought there was something about that voice. Even in a whisper, it reminded Hector—

"Give it to me! Hand it over, and I'll let you go." The kidnapper sounded angry, and shoved Hector so hard he fell on his side.

"You want that scrap of paper I picked up and put in my backpack near Dr. Graves' apartment, right? What is it, anyway?" Hector said, his voice shaking.

"You're safe if you don't know. Which pocket?"

"The outside."

Hector could hear the kidnapper searching

through his backpack. A whole bunch of stuff fell on the floor.

"Okay. I've got it. I've also got your wallet and your keys. So stop playing detective, or you'll be real sorry!"

"I will. I promise. I'll just sell my Jumbo Bars. Nothing else."

"Good." The voice was hoarse. "Because I have your stuff now. I can plant it somewhere on my next job, and bring you down with me."

"Honest! I'm done! No more questions. If people pay water bills, that's their business."

The minute the words were out of his mouth, Hector wished he could breathe them back in again. The kidnapper grabbed the front of Hector's shirt and pulled it so hard that his wrists strained against the ropes holding them to the post. "I thought you said you didn't look at what you took."

His neck ached from the shaking. He could feel the pain pounding in his head.

"I—I didn't look at it," Hector stammered. "I know about the water bills because I talked to Mr. Yafa and some of his friends. They were feeling real bad. They said somebody came to their door and made them pay a big bill. Now they don't have any money, and they don't know what to do about it. That's all I know."

Hector felt the gag being put back on. The kidnapper shoved him back against the post. "Okay, kid. You're lucky I'm so softhearted. I'm not going to hurt you this time. But you'd better stay away from me."

The kidnapper was so close, Hector could practically feel the breath on his face. It was creepy! Then Hector got a whiff of something. Something familiar. A good smell, but he couldn't quite identify it. It was kind of sweet, and kind of like mud. But before he could tell what the smell was, his Mets cap was yanked off his head.

He heard the kidnapper heading for the door and breathed a sigh of relief. Then he heard footsteps returning and the sounds of the kidnapper picking up Hector's plastic bag of Jumbo Bars and again moving toward the door. This time Hector could hear the sound of a candy bar wrapper being torn off as the door opened and closed. "I know someone who can use these," the kidnapper said, and laughed. Hector could hear the laughter echoing as if the kidnapper were still right there, breathing that sweet mud smell near his face.

When the rest of the team got to Dr. Graves' building, they found Hector's casebook lying on the ground in front of the entrance. It was open, pages down in the dirt, as if it had been dropped suddenly. Nearby there was a Jumbo Bar wrapper.

"Maybe Hector got mugged, and the casebook and that Jumbo Bar wrapper fell out of his backpack." Gaby shivered as she thought about it.

"We can't just sit here," Alex said, running a hand nervously through his thick, dark hair.

Casey started crying.

Jamal stroked Casey's head. "We have to be calm. If anyone can find Hector, it's Ghostwriter." He began to write.

It was quiet now where Hector was. He was finally alone. But he was more scared than he'd ever been in his life. He decided to count to 100 before he tried to move. Then he remembered that he couldn't move at all. His legs and hands were still tied up.

Use your brain, Hector, he told himself, trying to stay calm. *Any knot can be loosened. Just work your left hand up and down and try to make it as thin as you can when you come to the rope.* His breath came hard and fast as he struggled with the knots.

He noticed he could still smell the odor that had been on the kidnapper's breath. It was clinging to the gag. But he couldn't tell what it was. At last Hector managed to loosen the knot on his left wrist enough to be able to reach the dusty floor. *That kidnapper must be an amateur,* Hector thought, trying to feel braver than he was. *This knot isn't very good at all.*

Hector ran his hand along the floor behind him. He managed to scrawl "Help" in the dust.

Ghostwriter found the word, and his glow rushed out the door like a ball of fire. Then Ghostwriter picked up the address on the building next door to the one where Hector was hidden. He raced on, carrying "Help" and the address to the rest of the team, outside Dr. Graves' building.

Suddenly the door banged open. Hector's gag was pulled off, and the ropes were untied. But the blindfold was still on.

"Who are you?" Hector wanted to know. He knew the team couldn't have found him this fast.

There was no answer. Hector reached up to the blindfold, but a hand stopped him. "Okay," said Hector. "You don't want me to see you, but whoever you are, thanks a lot. I really thought I was done for."

Still there was no answer. Just a quick scurrying and a draft of cool air as the door opened and closed. Hector didn't know what to do. *Suppose it's some kind of trick,* he thought, *and the person who untied me is just another member of the gang?* Maybe they were waiting outside with a car that would run Hector over as he left the abandoned building!

The best thing seemed to be to wait until he knew for sure he was alone. It was the loneliest five minutes of Hector's life—and the longest.

Chapter 7

Escape!

Casey saw Ghostwriter's glow coming first and pointed to the message that was flying though the air like skywriting: 537 Washington Street. Help!

"Let's go!" shouted Tina. They took off.

Meanwhile, Hector couldn't wait one more minute. He counted to ten, pulled off the blindfold, and looked around. He expected to find himself in a warehouse or a basement hideout, but instead he saw that he was in a tumbledown abandoned store. He could see what used to be shelves and counters and windows, which were dirty but not broken.

Hector wanted to get out fast, before the kidnapper came back. Once on the street, he was shocked to see where he was—the corner of Washington and Lafayette, just a couple of blocks from Gaby and Alex's bodega.

Hector looked for a pay phone to call the police, but when he found one it was out of order. He decided to head for his apartment, where he hoped to find the team. He pictured how great it would be to see them again when . . . the team came sprinting around the corner! Gaby and Casey threw their arms around him. Casey wanted to know how he'd gotten so dirty, and they all shouted questions.

"Where have you been?"

"We waited for ages—and then Ghostwriter sent us a 'help' message."

"Are you okay?"

"I was tied up and blindfolded. Some kid got me loose," Hector said. There was a stunned silence for a moment, and then the team started shouting more questions.

"Well, I've got plenty to tell you," Hector began, but then he realized he had never been so hungry in his whole life. "Could we go back to your house and get something to eat?" Hector asked Alex. "Then I'll explain everything."

Back at Alex and Gaby's, Alex handed Hector a cheese sandwich, some chips, and a cold soda. "Poor Hector," said Tina, watching him eat. For a minute Hector thought this was pretty great, everyone feeling sorry for him. But then he remembered what it had been like being kidnapped, and knew he wouldn't go through that again, not for all the chips and sympathy in New York City!

"Come on," Jamal said. "You can feed your face later. Tell us what happened."

"Well, when Gaby and Casey left me, I tried to sell a Jumbo Bar to Dr. Graves, but I couldn't get anywhere with her. So I started to leave, and I bumped into some woman—I think it was a woman. It was all so fast."

"You're as bad as the Lunch Bunch," said Gaby. "Didn't you notice anything about this person?"

"That's what got me in trouble," Hector continued. "I was thinking about my Jumbo Bars so much I didn't look where I was going, and then this clumsy person knocked my whole bag of bars out of my hands. While I was picking up the candy I found a piece of paper and stuffed it in my backpack pocket. I think that's why I was kidnapped. That piece of paper was a water bill, made out to Dr. Graves!"

"You must have been scared out of your wits," Tina said.

Hector's mouth was full, but he shook his head. He swallowed and went on. "It must have been a big person. I was attacked from behind and bundled up and carried away before I could defend myself."

"We know you did the best you could," Lenni said.

"Did this kidnapper speak with an accent like all the con artists?" asked Gaby.

"The person kept whispering. It seemed like a woman but I'm still not sure. I couldn't figure out what the accent was. It was like there was a different voice every time. Like he or she was playing lots of different parts."

"Or maybe there were a couple of gang members there," Casey guessed.

"No, there was just one in the abandoned store. I'm sure of that now. I heard only one set of footsteps when the person left." Hector thought for a minute. "However differently that kidnapper talked, there was something about the voice. I think I might know that voice. But I just can't place it."

"Let's assume there was just one person, then, and it was most likely a woman," Tina said. "When you bumped into her in the hallway, what do you remember about her?"

"She was old. I think she was old. Something about the way she walked." Hector was doing his best to remember. "That's why I think the person in the building might have been different from the one who kidnapped me outside. The one who tied me up and questioned me didn't move like an old person at all. She was strong!"

"So maybe we have a man pretending to be a woman." Gaby was making notes as she talked. "Or a woman who sometimes pretends she's a man. An old person who's very strong and active, or a younger one who can act like an old person."

Jamal shook his head. "You aren't giving us much to go on, Hector."

"I'm trying. I just can't remember anything special."

"Think about it for a minute," Tina suggested. "Sometimes you can remember details by just sitting quietly and remembering what you were doing."

Hector tried to do what Tina said. "First I was walking down the hall from Dr. Graves'. I bumped into someone and I found a water bill on the floor. Then I rode the elevator back down to the first floor. I was walking home when someone grabbed me from behind, tied me up, and blindfolded me. That must have been when the casebook fell out of my backpack."

All of a sudden, Hector looked up. "There was something in the abandoned store. It was when the kidnapper put the gag back on me the second time. When the kidnapper got close to me—it was a smell I knew. It was—wait a minute—it was chocolate!"

"Oh, boy!" Gaby slammed her notebook shut. "You have Jumbo Bars on the brain."

"Yes! That's the other thing! The kidnapper left, but then came back for my bag of Jumbo Bars."

"You see what I mean?" Gaby was disgusted with Hector.

"I'm telling you what I mean." Hector gobbled up another handful of chips. "I smelled chocolate. Come on, you guys. How do we always know when Casey's made one of her food raids? We smell the peanut butter coming before we even see her."

Hector grinned at Casey, and she giggled. But the rest of the team nodded in agreement.

"Okay," Jamal said. "You might have some real evidence there. It means something, but I'm not sure what."

Gaby wrote "chocolate breath" in the "Other Clues" list in the casebook.

"You were in real danger, Hector," Alex said. "And I was so scared that you were hurt I didn't know what to do. We have to solve this case before someone else gets in trouble. We have to find out who's pulling this scam on the Lunch Bunch and threatening us."

"So, who do we have as suspects?" Jamal asked, opening the casebook to the "Suspects" section and adding new evidence:

SUSPECT
Keisha

EVIDENCE
Was volunteer at Lunch Bunch so could have list
Fliers left at apartments

SUSPECT
Conrad, the Lunch Bunch van driver

EVIDENCE
He has the Lunch Bunch list
The mystery kid mentioned him
Seen talking to Lunch Bunch customer who was crying

SUSPECT
Assistant X

EVIDENCE
Works on van so has Lunch Bunch list

There was a long silence. Then Lenni spoke up. "We haven't found out anything about Assistant X, the kid who volunteers with Conrad."

"We don't know much about Conrad, either. Except that Hector saw him at the door of that woman who was crying. That mystery kid wrote in a note that he's probably not the one, but I'm not sure I believe it," Jamal said.

"We know Conrad works in a theater and teaches acting," said Gaby. "Maybe he's using a bunch of his actor friends to do these cons."

"Let's go interview Conrad tomorrow. Maybe Assistant X will be with him and we can get two interviews," said Alex.

"We should also talk to Keisha," said Tina. "We need more evidence about her, too."

"I'll tell you what we have to do now," said Alex. "We have to tell Hector's mother and the police what happened to Hector today."

"Wait a minute," said Hector, who was already feeling better. "That would be the end of the Jumbo Candy Bar Contest for me if my mom found out I was *kidnapped.* And didn't you already say the police just think we're playing a prank?"

Alex and Jamal exchanged doubtful looks.

"Just give me one more day to sell some chocolate," said Hector. "Then I'll tell her myself."

"Weeell, okay," said Alex, but he looked unsure.

The team agreed to meet at the bodega at nine o'clock the next morning. Before they split up, Alex asked if anyone wanted a drink. Hector said he wanted lemonade and Lenni and Jamal asked for sodas.

When Alex came back with the drinks, he was waving a piece of paper at the team.

"Look at this, guys," he said. "I found it stuck in an empty bottle in the recycling area outside. It says: 'To catch the con, go see Mrs. Salazar tomorrow afternoon at two o'clock.'"

"The handwriting looks the same as the other notes we got from the mystery kid," Hector pointed out. "The mystery kid is trying to help us."

"Either that—or this kid is part of the scam," said Lenni. "We've got to find out."

By nine o'clock the next morning, the whole team had gathered at the bodega. Jamal was holding the note left by the mystery kid the night before. "I don't get it," he said. "How does the mystery kid know so much about this con job?"

"Maybe Ghostwriter could help us figure it out," said Gaby. She took the note from Jamal and wrote on it, "Who wrote this, Ghostwriter? We have to find out fast." Ghostwriter's glow whirled out and came back in seconds, with these words: June 15th—I hope Hector is all right. I tried to help him.

"This looks like another diary entry," Alex said.

"And like the other notes we've gotten," Hector said excitedly. "But how does this person know I was in danger? Could this be the person who saved me yesterday?"

"This is getting weirder and weirder," said Alex.

"What do you remember about the person who untied you?" Tina asked Hector.

"All I know is it seemed like a kid," Hector said. "The hands weren't big."

"We still don't know enough to find this person," Tina said, frustrated.

Ghostwriter suddenly flew out of the room as if he had a bright idea. When he returned, his message left the team even more confused.

Roberto Kelly—CF

"What's a CF?" Lenni wanted to know. Casey piped up immediately with the answer: "Center field. Roberto Kelly is a center fielder with the Cincinnati Reds." You could count on Casey to know everything in the world about baseball.

"But what does that have to do with this case?" Alex asked. The kids were really stumped.

"It's a clue," Gaby said, writing it under "Other Clues" in the casebook. "An important clue. But what does it mean?

"Hey, this is weird," Gaby said after she finished writing. "Look what we already had under 'Other Clues.'" She held up the book and pointed to a section that said:

The Blaster
ERA 3.50
HAIR: Brown
EYES: Brown

"It's the writing Ghostwriter found around Mr. Yafa's water bill back when the case first started," said Alex. "But what do baseball and water bills have in common?"

Ghostwriter was back again, filling the air in the bodega with more names and batting averages of baseball players.

"More baseball cards?" Casey asked.

"Maybe the con artist has a huge collection of baseball cards," said Hector.

"Mrs. Astor's store is full of trading cards and more than half of them are baseball cards," said Casey. "Maybe we should check it out."

"Yeah," said Hector, thinking hard. "I'm ninety-nine percent sure this mystery kid who keeps writing to us is the kid who always hangs out at Mrs. Astor's store. I remember it seemed like that kid—I couldn't tell if it was a boy or a girl—was listening in on my talks with Mrs. Astor. And Ghostwriter showed me one message that seemed to come right from the kid's backpack."

"Listen, you guys," Alex said. "This is serious stuff. We have to tell Hector's mom what happened. And we have to tell the police, too. And this time I mean it. Let's just hope that Lieutenant McQuade is back in the office. I don't want to talk to that other guy again."

"We're leaving, Papa!" Alex shouted so that Mr. Fernandez, who was stacking cans in the storeroom at the back of the bodega, could hear him.

As they opened the door to leave, the phone rang. Gaby ran back and answered it. "It's for you, Hector," she called. "Perfect timing! It's your mom."

Hector took the phone.

"Hector," his mother said, "some police officers

were just here. They said they needed to ask you some questions."

"What kind of questions?" Hector asked. He hadn't even told them yet he had been kidnapped!

"They said someone called them about a con artist trying to rip off people in the neighborhood. And when they went to investigate, some of your stuff was found at the front door of one of the victims."

"Oh, no!" groaned Hector. The color drained out of his face. "I don't believe it!"

"This policeman wants us to meet him at the station. What's this all about, Hector? Have you gotten into some kind of trouble?"

"No, Mama, don't worry. We can work it all out." But when Hector hung up a minute later, he didn't look so sure.

"What's wrong?" all the team asked at once.

"The police found my stuff near one of the apartments that the con artist hit. I bet it's the stuff that kidnapper took from me. My mom's coming to meet me here and we have to go to the police station right away." Hector tried to hide how scared he had become, but his voice was shaking when he asked the team, "Do you think I'll be sent to prison?"

Chapter 8

Hector's Nightmare

The next thing Hector knew, he and his mother were walking up the steps of the police station. Hector felt weak in the knees, but he was glad to see that the team had raced there to meet him.

Casey looked as if she might cry. That made Hector feel braver. At the door a police officer came and told Hector his friends would have to wait outside.

"Go on," Hector told the team. "I'll be okay. You guys would help me more if you went on trying to find the con artist."

When Hector and his mother got inside, they were told that Lieutenant McQuade was out on a case and Detective Murray would see Hector. Detective Murray led Hector and his mother to a smaller room.

Hector wanted to be as friendly as he could, so he offered the big detective a Jumbo Bar. The detective said no.

"This isn't a social gathering," Detective Murray said.

"You don't think I have anything to do with the fake water bills, do you?" Hector asked. "Lieutenant McQuade knows me. He knows how many cases I've helped solve."

"As a matter of fact, I haven't discussed the case with Lieutenant McQuade. What's important here is that we have evidence that points to you as a part of this scam. If you can explain how all these pieces fit together, you will be free to leave."

"Can I at least talk to the lieutenant? A terrible thing happened to me yesterday that he should know about," Hector said. His mother flashed him a worried look but stayed quiet.

The detective shrugged. "We'll see. Sit down, Hector."

"No thanks," said Hector. "I'll stand." He'd seen guys do that on TV. He didn't know why they did it, but it made Hector feel a little bit more in control.

"We have some evidence here that we want you to

explain," Detective Murray began. "Have you ever seen these things before?" He shoved a Mets cap, a wallet, and some keys across the table toward Hector.

"Sure. That's the stuff the kidnapper took from me."

"Kidnapper?" One of Detective Murray's eyebrows shot up. Hector's mother gasped.

"I was finding out too much about the water bill scam. And I found a piece of real evidence," Hector said. "So someone kidnapped me and told me to keep quiet. And then the kidnapper took all my stuff."

"What evidence? Where is the evidence now?" Detective Murray was scowling.

"The kidnapper took it back."

The detective sighed. "Why would somebody kidnap you and then take this stuff? I guess I could understand the wallet—except you don't carry any credit cards, and you only had a few dollars. I could even believe the part about the keys. Maybe they were planning a break-in. But your Mets cap? Why would anyone want your cap?"

"I don't know. Maybe the kidnapper wanted a Mets cap for their kid?"

"Hector, let's get serious. The cap was found about ten feet away from Mrs. Dowling's door. And this was found hanging on the door. Your keys were found by Mrs. Eisen's door, where there was another

of these tags with your name and phone number."
The detective threw one of Hector's hangtags onto
the table.

"I put the tags on their doors to get orders. Mrs.
Eisen wasn't home yesterday afternoon, but I was
going back today. But I never got there. I was kidnapped!" Hector knew his story sounded pretty suspicious. He didn't know how to make the detective
believe he was telling the truth.

"You'll be interested to know that Mrs. Dowling
was home yesterday afternoon. She paid a four-hun-
dred-fifty-dollar water bill!"

"Did she see the con artist?"

"Her description was as confused as all the
others."

"I don't get it, Detective Murray, except that when
the kidnapper took my stuff, she—I'm pretty sure it
was a she—she said she would use it to bring me
down with her. I guess that's what she's been trying to
do." Hector took a big breath and let it out in a sigh.
"And it looks like her plan is working pretty well."

The detective was losing his patience. "Just now,
when you came into the station, Mrs. Eisen was at
the entrance."

"Why?" Hector asked.

"We wanted her to identify you. She said she saw
you in her hallway right before the bill collector
came."

"Well, sure, I was there. I was trying to see if she wanted to buy some candy! She only lives a couple of doors down the hall from Dr. Graves. Alex, Casey, Gaby, and I thought the next scam would be at Dr. Graves' apartment, so we staked it out all day yesterday."

"Did you see the bill collector go to Dr. Graves'?"

"Yes—well, no, not exactly. That was when I got kidnapped."

Detective Murray got up and walked around the table to the side where Hector was. He perched on the edge of the table and crossed his arms across his chest. "People are saying they think you case apartments while you go around selling those Jumbo Bars. And if a single older person lives there you hang one of these on the door."

Detective Murray dangled the tag in front of Hector. "We think it's a signal. If the con artists see it on the door, they know it's a good apartment to try the scam."

"That's not true," Hector protested. "I wouldn't do anything like that. Ask Lieutenant McQuade, he knows me."

"That's not all we have, though. Dr. Graves says this wallet was dropped in front of her apartment. When did you lose your wallet, Hector?"

"I told you. I didn't lose it. The kidnapper took it."

"This kidnapping story of yours is pretty far-fetched. What proof do you have?"

Hector was scared. Detective Murray seemed tough, and Hector knew he was getting in deeper and deeper trouble. Just then Ghostwriter flashed in and rearranged the letters on a crime prevention poster on the wall: **Hang in there, Hector.** It gave Hector a burst of strength.

"For one thing, you've got all my stuff. I mean, would I really put my wallet next door to somebody I was going to rob? Would I be so careless that I would drop all these things in one day and not miss them? How could I lose my cap without knowing it was gone?"

"What you say makes sense, Hector, but it isn't proof."

Suddenly Hector's eyes brightened as he had an idea. Why hadn't he thought of this before? "I've got a witness! The kid who untied me."

"Who's that?"

"I don't know. The kid wouldn't talk, and I was blindfolded."

The detective shook his head. "You seem to have an answer for everything, Hector. Right now I'd say you're in pretty big trouble. You can go for now, but I'd say the chances are good you're going to end up in juvenile court if you don't start coming clean."

"Can you give me one day to prove I'm innocent?" Hector pleaded.

Detective Murray looked hard at Hector. "I'll be using that day to look into this further. You can go now."

The minute they stepped from the room, Hector's mother hugged him hard.

"Come on, *hijo*," she said, "We're going home and you're explaining everything. I'm just going to have to miss work."

"Please, Mama, if you ever trusted me, trust me now. I'll be okay—I promise. And you know you can't miss work!" Mrs. Carrero looked doubtful, but finally she kissed Hector. "We have a *long* talk coming, Hector, but if you say you didn't do anything bad, I believe you. Stay out of trouble until I get home, you hear?" The two walked outside, where the team was waiting. Mrs. Carrero kissed Hector again. "You boys keep an eye on Hector," she said to Jamal and Alex. She headed down the steps.

"It's not over yet," Hector explained to the team after she was gone. "I've got only one day to prove I'm innocent before they officially accuse me of being part of a con game to cheat old people. And Detective Murray said I could wind up in juvenile court."

"There's only one way to handle this," Lenni said. "We have to solve the case."

"Great," Hector said shaking his head sadly. "That gives us until tomorrow night at the latest. Right now, we aren't even close."

"Oh, man," Alex said, looking at his watch. "It's eleven-twenty. I've *got* to go work in the bodega. Sorry, Hector. But I'll help later."

"Well, the rest of us can get going," Jamal said. "Hector, Tina, and I'll go talk to Conrad and Assistant X."

"I'll talk to Keisha," Gaby volunteered. Lenni and Casey said they'd go with her.

"Let's meet at the bodega after we see all our suspects," Lenni said. "Then all of us can go to Mrs. Astor's to check out the baseball card clues."

"And don't forget that note we got from the mystery kid," said Hector. "It said we should stake out Mrs. Salazar's today at two o'clock."

The team knew they didn't have a moment to lose!

Jamal, Tina, and Hector found Conrad's van parked in front of Dr. Graves' building, but nobody was inside. After a few minutes, Conrad came out the front door, mopping his face with his bandanna and cursing under his breath. The three kids walked up to him.

"Excuse me, we need to ask you a few questions," said Jamal.

"Like what?" Conrad said with a sneer. He unlocked

the van door and reached in for a Jumbo almond bar that had been sitting on the dashboard.

"What are you, kid detectives?" Conrad had a slight German accent.

"He eats Jumbo almond bars. And he has an accent," Hector whispered to Tina as he opened the casebook and started taking notes.

Jamal began the questioning. "That candy looks good. Where did you get it?"

"Bought it from some kid," Conrad said.

"From the kid who works with you?" Jamal asked.

Conrad's neck and ears turned red.

"Don't get me started on that kid! Talk about worthless! On the first day, the address list is lost. And now, when it's a hundred degrees out and we have fifty lunches to deliver, where is the kid? Off buying baseball cards, probably. I'm better off working by myself. That's the trouble with volunteers. You can't depend on them."

Jamal changed the subject. He told Conrad about the water bill scam and asked him if he knew anything about it.

Conrad was insulted. "I'm too busy getting all these meals delivered to scam anybody. These people are my *friends*."

"Someone saw you early yesterday morning, at an old woman's apartment, and she was crying. How come?" Hector asked.

This time Conrad really blew his stack. "It's none of your business!" he bellowed. He stopped for a quick breath and then went on, "These people are like my family; why would I bother them? Now get lost, before I lose my temper and do something I'll regret!"

Jamal and Tina didn't need another warning. But Hector couldn't resist the chance to sell a Jumbo Bar.

"I noticed you like Jumbo Bars. Want to buy some more?" Hector asked.

Conrad glared at Hector. "You sell them? I only eat the almond ones."

Hector searched through his backpack.

"Sorry, no almond. How about peanut butter?"

Conrad looked disgusted. "Forget it. Leave me alone. Go join your friends."

Hector remembered one last question.

"Could you just tell me the name of your assistant and where the kid lives?"

Conrad had had enough. "Why are you kids so nosy? Scram!"

Hector ran to catch up with Jamal and Tina.

"Well, that didn't help," Hector said glumly. "We didn't learn anything new."

Things weren't going much better for Gaby, Lenni, and Casey. Keisha wouldn't talk to them if there were any customers around, and they had to wait several minutes.

When Keisha did talk, it was clear that she disliked Hector just as much as he disliked her. "With Hector, anything's possible. I'm not surprised the police are suspicious."

"Do you know anything about the Lunch Bunch? Didn't you used to volunteer there?" Gaby asked.

"Sure I did. But I don't now. And I don't go around selling my candy door-to-door. I do it right out on the street where everybody can see what I'm doing," Keisha said with her nose in the air. "I passed out fliers, but those just told people where they could find my candy stand."

Keisha turned away, making it clear she was done talking. Lenni wrote down everything she had said. But it didn't seem like much.

Chapter 9

On the Hunt

It was one o'clock, and the team was gathered at the bodega, trying to figure out a plan. They knew if they couldn't find the con artists by tomorrow, Hector would be in big trouble. The team knew it had to solve the case for the Lunch Bunch, too.

"Well, if the message from the mystery kid is right, we should get ourselves to Mrs. Salazar's by two o'clock," Alex said.

"We've got one hour," Jamal said. "Let's go over what we found out today and then head over to Mrs. Astor's like we planned."

"Look!" Casey said, pointing at the casebook, which was sitting on the counter by the cash register.

Ghostwriter was reviewing the evidence! First the whole book glowed orange and sparkled; then the words on each page showed up on the outside, just for a second, before they were replaced by the words on the next page.

"Wouldn't it be cool to be able to read that fast?" Lenni said.

"Yeah," said Hector, "but I'd rather not try being a ghost until I have to!"

Ghostwriter sent them a message: **Let's review only the suspects the team has seen.** He lit them up in the air:

> SUSPECT
> Keisha
>
> EVIDENCE
> Was volunteer at Lunch Bunch so could have list
> Fliers left at apartments
>
>
> SUSPECT
> Conrad, the Lunch Bunch van driver
>
> EVIDENCE
> He has the Lunch Bunch list
> The mystery kid mentioned him

Seen talking to Lunch Bunch cus-
tomer who was crying
Slender
Has German accent

SUSPECT
Assistant X

EVIDENCE
Works on van so has Lunch Bunch
list
Likes baseball cards

Alex put a big red question mark on the "Suspect"
page next to "Assistant X." "We've *got* to find a way
to check that kid out," he said.

Hector's mind was a million miles away. He pictured himself in handcuffs being led off to jail,
yelling all the way that he was innocent. He imag-
ined Keisha standing at her table waving a Jumbo
Bar at him in triumph as he rode by in a police car.
He could even hear his mother sobbing, "Oh, *hijo*,
why, *why?*"

"Hector." Gaby nudged him. "Wake up. We're
trying to help you and there isn't much time."

Hector nodded, glad for the millionth time that
he had such great friends.

Lenni looked at her watch. "We have just enough

time to check out Mrs. Astor's shop. We can see if her baseball cards give us a clue. Then we'll go to Mrs. Salazar's."

"Let's go!" Casey was on the case!

When they got to Mrs. Astor's shop, there was a large sign in the window: BIG SALE—20 TO 50% OFF ALL BASEBALL CARDS. Of course the shop was full of kids, and there were lots of others on the street waiting to get in. Even Keisha had taken time off from selling Jumbo Bars to go to the sale.

While they were waiting to get in, Hector decided to do a little business himself. He sold a couple of bars to the kids waiting in line.

Hector looked around, trying to find the kid with the Mets cap who was always hanging around and listening to his conversations. The big attraction was a box of baseball cards in the center of the tiny shop. Kids pushed each other out of the way so that they could see what was on sale.

Mrs. Astor was lining the kids up and jotting orders on a pad. "Look how sharp she is," said Lenni. "I always thought of Mrs. Astor as kind of flaky."

Jamal was trying to push his way to Mrs. Astor to ask where the baseball card kid was. When he got to her, though, she had no time for him.

The team split up and snooped around, trying to talk to any kid with a Mets cap on, but that didn't tell them much either.

After about fifteen minutes, the box of cards was empty. The sale was over and kids melted away like ice in summer.

"Can we talk to you now, Mrs. Astor?" Alex asked.

"Make it fast. There's a big Mets game at Shea Stadium at two o'clock. I have to catch it so I'm closing at one-thirty," she said. "Hector, give me one of those good peanut butter Jumbo Bars to have on the way."

As Mrs. Astor took the money out of her register to pay Hector, Casey pulled Gaby out of the shop. "There's no Mets game today. I'm sure they're playing out of town," Casey said. She checked the Mets schedule she always carried with her, and she was right. "Isn't that weird?" Casey said. "Why would Mrs. Astor lie about that?"

In the shop, Mrs. Astor opened the candy and took a big bite. Then she paid Hector and gave him a playful hug.

Hector and the rest of the team left the store and joined Casey and Gaby outside. Right away, Hector noticed Conrad walking on the other side of the street and decided to try for a Jumbo Bar sale. Hector figured he might also gather more evidence, since Conrad was still a suspect.

"I couldn't help but notice that you like Jumbo Bars. Do you want to buy one from me?" asked Hector, smiling.

"Okay," Conrad grumbled. "But it has to be one of the almond ones." Hector smiled. Maybe he could catch up with Keisha after all.

Conrad already had the candy bar open and was on his second bite while Hector was making change. Suddenly Hector slapped his forehead. He'd figured it out. He knew who the con artist was.

Hector practically threw Conrad's change at him and raced back across the street to the team.

"What's the matter with you?" Gaby asked.

Hector flagged down a taxi and dragged the team inside. "We have to get to Lieutenant McQuade's, fast," he told them, and the cab sped off before Hector could even explain to the team what he had figured out.

At Lieutenant McQuade's apartment, Mrs. McQuade answered the door. "I have to see Lieutenant McQuade," Hector said excitedly.

"I'm sorry, Hector. He's had the flu and he's taking a little nap right now," Mrs. McQuade said, motioning for Hector and the team to be quiet.

"This is urgent. We have to stop a crime!" Hector yelled.

Lieutenant McQuade was in pajamas when he came to the door, rubbing his eyes. "What's going on, honey?" he asked.

"I'm sorry. Hector says he has to see you. That it's urgent."

"It's okay, hon. I'll take care of it."

Hector poured out his story to Lieutenant McQuade—the water bill scam, the mysterious notes, being kidnapped, being called into the police station.

"I just found out something that I think could solve the case. But we need you to come with us, right away, to Mrs. Salazar's apartment."

Lieutenant McQuade looked tired—and doubtful.

"We weren't going to bother you," Hector continued. "We were going to try to stake it out ourselves. But now you have to come with us. I know who the con artist is, and you can make an arrest."

"Take it easy, Hector. How do you know who'll be at Mrs. Salazar's? From what you've told me, we're dealing with a dangerous gang."

"No gang. Just one person. I'd stake my life on it."

"What evidence do you have?" The lieutenant was interested now. He trusted Hector—and the whole team.

"A smell."

"What are you talking about? Some kind of perfume or aftershave lotion or something?"

"No. Jumbo Bars."

"*What?*"

Hector opened a bar and held it under Lieutenant McQuade's nose. "Smell that."

"Wow! That is a potent odor." The lieutenant shoved the bar back at Hector.

"Exactly. That smell was on my kidnapper's

breath," Hector said. "And I smelled the same thing today when I got close to the con artist."

"So who is it?"

Hector looked around. He took a notepad off the lieutenant's desk and wrote down a name with his Ghostwriter pen.

When the lieutenant saw the name, he whistled. "You're sure?" Hector nodded. "Okay. I'll come with you to Mrs. Salazar's."

Chapter 10

A Heart Attack

On the way to Mrs. Salazar's, Lieutenant McQuade called for backup. He and the team drove to meet Officer Tao. It was ten to two when the two police cars pulled up a block away from Mrs. Salazar's apartment building. The kids and Officer Tao followed Lieutenant McQuade to Mrs. Salazar's apartment.

Lieutenant McQuade called in to her, "It's the police, Mrs. Salazar. Open the door." At first Mrs. Salazar wouldn't open the door. The police continued to knock and call Mrs. Salazar's name.

Finally they heard a bolt being pulled back, and another one, and a chain being unfastened before the door opened. Mrs. Salazar looked them over and said, "Okay. Come in. What do you want?"

The lieutenant explained that he had reason to believe that a con artist would be coming to give her a water bill sometime soon.

"If you just stay calm, Mrs. Salazar, and do as I tell you, everything will be all right," Lieutenant McQuade assured her. "The same goes for you kids. I don't want anybody playing hero."

The team agreed. They were just glad the lieutenant was letting them in on the end of this case.

"Everyone but Hector and Mrs. Salazar, go into the next room. Sit out of the line of sight, and don't say anything. I don't want you in here before I make my arrest. It might be dangerous if the suspect is armed."

"Hector, I want you to listen to the con artist and nod if it's the voice you know."

"Right, Lieutenant."

The kids all took their places. Officer Tao and Lieutenant McQuade stood on either side of the door. Hector stood near Mrs. Salazar, but he made sure the con artist wouldn't be able to see him. They didn't have to wait long.

At two o'clock, they heard footsteps coming down the hall. As the sound came closer and closer, the group in Mrs. Salazar's apartment became more and more tense.

Then the doorbell rang. Mrs. Salazar answered with a tremble in her voice, "Who's there?"

"New York City Accounting Department." It sounded like a woman, but it was hard to tell. She had a strong Irish accent, so the words were hard to make out.

"I don't understand," said Mrs. Salazar. She looked at McQuade for help. McQuade looked at Hector, who nodded vigorously.

"I've got a bill that you must pay. We have to talk," said the voice. "A bill for your water."

That's all McQuade needed. He signaled Mrs. Salazar to open the door. She did, and a person standing in the shadows of the hallway handed her what looked like a water bill.

As Mrs. Salazar took the paper, the con artist said, "It seems you owe the City a good deal of money—"

"Stay where you are," Lieutenant McQuade said, stepping forward and showing his badge. "Police—you're under arrest."

As the con artist moved forward out of the dark hallway, McQuade handcuffed her. It was Mrs. Astor, just as Hector had expected.

Mrs. Astor tried to pull her wrist away from McQuade, but he had a good grip.

"Aaaah!" she screamed in anger. The sound sent chills down Hector's spine.

As McQuade pulled Mrs. Astor into the apartment, she caught sight of Hector standing against the wall. Her eyes grew wide and she gasped.

"You little meddler," she shrieked. "You little *brat*! Didn't your mother ever teach you to mind your own business?"

McQuade gave her wrist a yank. "That's enough," he said. He read Mrs. Astor her rights as he pulled her arms behind her and snapped on a pair of handcuffs.

Mrs. Astor was starting to calm down. She looked at Hector again.

"I had the perfect scam going until you came into my shop and shot your mouth off. Your little speech about your poor old friends clued me in that you and your 'detective' pals were snooping around. To throw you off, I started collecting from the beginning of the list instead of the end. Then I switched again."

While Officer Tao held Mrs. Astor's arm, Lieutenant McQuade went into the next room and told the team they could come out.

"Why did you do it?" Lenni asked. "You live here. You know everyone."

"I needed the money," Mrs. Astor said. "Did you think I could pay my rent and eat by selling baseball cards?"

"I don't get it." Jamal had the casebook open. "There were so many different descriptions. Man, woman, tall, short, and the accents—people thought you were French or Hispanic. How could one person be described so many different ways?"

Mrs. Astor grinned at them all. "All my disguises—all my accents! I am a brilliant actress, don't you think? Too good for Broadway. Every time I was in a play, I *was* the part. When it was over, no one remembered it was me, and I had to wait months and months for the next role. So I decided to put my talent to better use. If I couldn't be a star, I could at least live the lifestyle I deserve to live."

As Mrs. Astor talked, her gray hair began to escape from under her black wig and swirl around her face. She started to laugh—first a cackle, and then a loud whoop.

She's crazy, Hector thought.

Suddenly her laughter stopped. She leaned against the wall. "Please. I'm sick. I think— Someone get me a doctor. Please!"

"Hey, Mrs. Astor!" Hector went over to her. Mrs. Astor looked very pale.

"Hector—I didn't mean to hurt you—" She gasped and could not finish her sentence.

"Lieutenant McQuade, I think she's really sick," Hector shouted.

The lieutenant unsnapped the handcuffs from one wrist and helped her sit on the sofa.

"Help me. Please." Mrs. Astor could barely get the words out.

Lieutenant McQuade went for the phone to call an ambulance, but as soon as he turned his back, Mrs. Astor jumped up and made a run for it. Lieutenant McQuade and Officer Tao were right after her, but it was amazing how fast she moved.

They raced down the stairs, and it looked as if Lieutenant McQuade was going to catch her, but at the last minute Mrs. Astor threw her pocketbook at him. He put his hand up to fend it off and stumbled, falling a few steps. Officer Tao tripped over him. That gave Mrs. Astor just enough room to burst out the door and rush down the busy sidewalk. She blended right into the crowd. By the time the police got outside, they couldn't see her. She had slipped right out of their grasp!

Suddenly the police saw a disturbance in the crowd.

"Over here, Lieutenant!" a kid shouted.

By now the whole team had come out to the street. They saw a kid grappling with an angry Mrs. Astor. They gave a cheer when Lieutenant McQuade ran over and handcuffed Mrs. Astor for the second time.

"Don't try any smart tricks," he growled. "You won't fool me again."

Officer Tao had gone to get the squad car, and she pulled up to the curb with the siren blaring and the lights flashing. Lieutenant McQuade put Mrs. Astor in the backseat before returning to his car and following Officer Tao to the station. The little crowd that had gathered drifted away.

"I can't believe it was *her*!" said Lenni. "She seemed like such a nice woman."

"I know," said Hector. "I thought she was my friend. Or at least I did until I finally remembered my kidnapper's breath smelled like the peanut butter Jumbo Bars Mrs. Astor was always eating."

"Well, we solved the case and we did it in time to save Hector," Jamal said. "That was some pretty good detective work we did."

"Mostly thanks to me and my nose," Hector said proudly.

"You? If it hadn't been for those mysterious notes, we wouldn't be anywhere." Lenni gave Hector a little swat on the head. "They told us where to go and when."

"They must have been from that kid who caught Mrs. Astor," Alex said, looking around for the kid.

"We have to figure out who the mystery kid is," said Casey. "Until we do the case won't be over."

"Whoever it was did some brave stuff. Rescuing Hector when he was kidnapped, sending us messages, and catching Mrs. Astor." Gaby was about to say more when a voice interrupted her.

Chapter 11

Hector Loses and Wins

"The hardest part was getting that note into Hector's backpack when he wasn't looking," said an unfamiliar voice. The team turned to see who it was. A ten-year-old girl with brown eyes and blondish-brown hair smiled shyly. It was the kid from Mrs. Astor's store, but this time she wore her Mets cap turned around backward so that her face showed.

"So you were the one who listened in when I told Mrs. Astor about Mr. Yafa, and how we do detective work? And then you followed me?" said Hector.

"Yup. I kept wanting to talk to you, but when I followed you, you'd avoid me," the girl answered.

"So you weren't part of the scam?" Lenni asked.

"No!" she said. "I was trying to help you stop it."

"How did you know we needed help?" Jamal asked.

"I didn't at first. Then I heard Hector talking about the team at Mrs. Astor's, and how you were all worried about Mr. Yafa. I figured you were trying to solve the case."

"Hold it," Hector said. "I'm starving. And we deserve a celebration. Let's go to the deli and get burgers and fries all around."

"Let's go!" Casey was already halfway up the block.

The rest of the team started to follow, but the girl turned to go in the other direction.

"Hey!" Gaby shouted. "You helped us solve this case, so you have to be part of the fun, too."

"We called you the mystery kid," Jamal said. "That's okay for a casebook, but you don't celebrate with somebody by that name. Who are you?"

"I'm Stephanie Zapalowicz. My friends call me Steph."

Everyone on the team introduced himself or herself.

"Okay, Steph," said Jamal, "get ready for the best burgers in the city of New York."

They all trooped into the restaurant and got their favorite table in the back. Casey decided to order a peanut butter sandwich. She said it was the right way to celebrate the case. Soon everyone was eating and talking.

"Let's start at the beginning," Alex said, turning to Stephanie. "I never saw you before. Are you from this neighborhood?"

"No, I'm not from around here. I live in Maryland. But I'm staying in Brooklyn for the summer, with friends of my family's. I just started volunteering with the Lunch Bunch program at the Community Center."

"You're kidding!" said Jamal. "So you help Conrad, the van driver?"

"You're Assistant X!" cried Tina. "We had you on our suspect list!"

Stephanie took a couple of fries and scooped up a big gob of ketchup. "It was great working with him at first. But then I lost the Lunch Bunch list and he got really mad at me. He's very moody."

"Tell us about it," said Hector. "How did you lose the list?"

"It turns out I didn't lose it. Mrs. Astor stole it. At first I couldn't figure it out. And I was getting worried, because bad things kept happening to the people on the list."

"Were you writing this all down in some kind of diary?" Alex interrupted.

"Yeah. I didn't know any kids yet. I had no one to talk to."

The team exchanged a secret smile. That diary must be what Ghostwriter had been reading when he sent those first messages.

"I looked everywhere for the list. Then I remembered that the last time I saw it was just before I went into Mrs. Astor's to look at the baseball cards. I'm really into baseball cards."

"You could have come to us, instead of slipping all those clues to us in secret," Casey said.

"I tried following Hector so I could talk to him. But boy, did he make it hard," Stephanie answered, looking at Hector and laughing. "One time, I was trying to catch up to him and he ran away like he'd just seen a ghost." Hector laughed, too, remembering how fast he had run.

"Another time, I was trying to catch up to him and these big guys thought he'd robbed me. So *they* took off after Hector. It got so I couldn't get near Hector without some disaster happening."

Everyone laughed. "Still," said Hector, "why didn't you go to the police?"

"I was sort of scared. At first I thought the whole thing was my fault. I thought if I went to the police, they would blame me. Later I thought I saw the list on Mrs. Astor's desk, and I really didn't know what to do!"

"Wow," Hector said. "It was really cool how you kept giving us clues."

"How did you know about Mrs. Salazar?" Jamal asked.

"By that time I was sure that Mrs. Astor was pulling the con. She'd already told me she was closing the store at one-thrity on Wednesday. Later when I saw a fake bill for Mrs. Salazar on her desk, I knew she would go straight to Mrs. Salazar's."

"I've got to know something important," said Hector. "Are you the one who rescued me when I was kidnapped?"

Stephanie took the last slurp of her drink and nodded.

"How did you know where I was?"

"That part's really weird. I was on my way to Mrs. Astor's when I saw her pushing a shopping cart crammed with blankets into an empty store. I thought something strange was going on, so I hung around to see what had happened.

"Then I saw Mrs. Astor come out and go into her own store." Stephanie hesitated. "I was about to leave when I saw the strangest thing happen. A kind of—I don't know how to describe it—it was like a ball of fire—whooshed out of the empty store."

"You saw it?" Hector was wide-eyed.

"Yeah, there was this whoosh, and then I saw a bunch of letters, *H-E-L-P*, go flying down the street.

It was the most incredible thing I ever saw. How did you do that?"

"You saw the letters?" Jamal was as stunned as Hector. In fact, the whole team was amazed. Ghostwriter had shown himself to Stephanie!

"So anyway, I realized that somebody was in trouble in there, so I went in and found Hector all tied up. I got him free, but I was scared Mrs. Astor would come back, so I just ran away."

"Wow! That was pretty brave to go in there," Lenni said.

"Yeah," Hector said. "You saved my life. No wonder Ghostwriter wrote to you."

"Ghostwriter? Who's that?" Stephanie asked.

Hector looked around the table. The other team members didn't look too happy about telling Stephanie about Ghostwriter. "But she saw him," Hector insisted.

Just then, sparkling stars, and letters started flying up from all the menus in the restaurant. Stephanie watched open-mouthed as a message formed in front of her.

Welcome to the team, Steph! You are a real hero!

Epilogue

"Let's go, Hector! We've got a big day."
Gaby tapped her foot impatiently while Hector ran
a comb through his hair.

Then they headed over to Lenni's loft, where the
rest of the team had rallied. They were all wearing
their best stuff, and Lenni had a wild new hat for
the occasion, with Olympic pins all over it.

Jamal had brought a cake, and Lenni had bought
juice. Tina had contributed some paper plates from
home, and Casey had laid everything out so that it
looked like a real party.

After they'd been there a while, though, Hector
looked pale. "I've got a stomachache," he moaned.

"I'm going home. I'll just have to miss all the excitement today."

"You don't look sick to me," Lenni said. "You just wolfed down *two* slices of Jamal's caramel cake and drank a big glass of juice."

"That's why I'm sick," Hector said in a whisper.

"Forget it. Missing the scholarship award I can understand. But we've got team business first. That's why we're having this rally. You have to be with us for that."

Hector nodded.

Just then someone rang the door buzzer.

"That's Steph," said Alex and went to let her in.

"What's up?" Stephanie asked. "I got a message to rally here. Are you guys on a new case? Can I help?"

"We had a couple of meetings about you," Jamal said, a serious expression on his face.

"What'd I do?" Stephanie looked alarmed.

"You saw Ghostwriter." Then Jamal couldn't keep the smile off his face. "You helped solve a very weird case. You saved Hector. You're a hero. And we want you to be one of us."

Jamal presented Stephanie with a team pen, and everyone cheered. Lenni told Stephanie that she couldn't tell anyone else about Ghostwriter, and explained how the team got started, and how they solved crimes.

Suddenly the magnetic letters on Lenni's refrigerator started spinning around. They hovered in midair and spelled out **Thanks for helping the team, Steph!**

"That's Ghostwriter!" said Casey. "Write something back!"

Stephanie was shy at first and couldn't think of anything.

"We all felt that way the first time," Hector encouraged her. "Just say what you feel."

She took a piece of paper and wrote with her new pen. "Thanks for letting me join the team. Now I almost wish I could stay here in Brooklyn forever. But when the summer's over, I'm going home to Maryland. Will you come visit me, Ghostwriter?"

Everyone looked up to see how Ghostwriter would reply. Everything was still for a moment and then letters gently floated up from the books on the coffee table:

Sure! I've always wanted to read what's up in Maryland!

The whole team put their hands in a pile and raised them in their special cheer: "G-h-o-o-o-s-t-writer!"

Then the team invited Stephanie to come with them to the Jumbo Bar award ceremony at the Community Center.

When they got there, the Community Center was

decked out as if it were the Fourth of July. Red, white, and blue streamers were all over the auditorium walls. Kids were talking to one another and yelling across the hall. Then Mrs. Malloy, the director of the center, cleared her throat to get everyone's attention.

Hector had been dreading this part. He slouched in his seat. Up on the stage along with the director of the Community Center sat Lieutenant McQuade, the president of the Jumbo Bar company, and, smiling ear to ear, Keisha. She was wearing her gymnastics leotard and had about a thousand pink ribbons in her hair.

"What an adorable little girl! So *sweet*," said a woman sitting behind the team. Hector groaned and slouched even lower in his chair.

"I'll make this short, I promise." Mrs. Malloy smiled. "The Jumbo Bar contest was a real success. We sold more bars than I thought the neighborhood could eat in a year." Everyone applauded, except for a couple of smart-aleck kids sitting in the back who made gagging noises. "As you know, Joshua Slocum, the president of the Jumbo Bar Company, is giving us a quarter for every bar sold so that we can buy new gym equipment." Everybody applauded again as Mr. Slocum took the microphone.

"We also promised a full scholarship to summer sports camp to the boy or girl who sold the most bars." Mr. Slocum smiled at Keisha. "At first it looked as if we'd end up with a tie and would be giving out two scholarships. But real salesmanship paid off, and I'm happy to give this award to Keisha Brock."

People clapped as Mr. Slocum presented Keisha with an envelope and a huge trophy of a Jumbo Bar. Keisha grinned and then did a big curtsy toward the audience. Everyone applauded, even Hector, although Casey thought she saw tears in his eyes.

Then, to everyone's surprise, Lieutenant McQuade held up his hands for quiet. "Wait. Wait. We're not done. We officers at the precinct had a meeting of our own, and then another one with Mr. Slocum. He agreed with us. The company does need to award two full scholarships this year after all.

"As you know, in the last week there has been a series of crimes against some of our older citizens. We were able to solve them only with the help of someone from this neighborhood who showed real courage and intelligence.

"So," the lieutenant went on, "it gives me real pleasure to present a special Jumbo Bar Scholarship to Hector Carrero."

The whole room started cheering, and then everyone stood up to cheer some more. Hector was so shocked he couldn't move. Jamal and Lenni nudged him. "Hector, you're supposed to go up there," Lenni whispered. As Hector walked toward the stage, he felt as if he were dreaming. He wasn't sure how he was managing to walk. Then it dawned on him: Hector Carrero was going to have a whole summer with the pros after all. He really might become an Olympic-class swimmer some day. "Ghostwriter," he said to himself as he raised his arms in a victory salute, "this one is for you."